Rascal
DOES NOT DREAM
of a
Lost
Singer

HAJIME
KAMOSHIDA

Illustration by
KEJI MIZOGUCHI

Mai Sakurajima

Her acting career is back in full swing. Her boyfriend, Sakuta, is attending the same college. Even as her work schedule picks up, she treasures her time with him.

Mai and Sakuta are in college now and starting new lives.

"Mai's mine, and you can't have her."

"Jealous!"

Sakuta Azusagawa

An unusual college freshman, he still doesn't own a phone. Worked hard to get into Mai's college and is settling into a happy life with her.

"Must be nice dating someone pretty. I wish I was!"

Miori Mitou

A beautiful college girl in Sakuta's class. She doesn't own a phone and is not easily dissuaded—she's declared herself a potential friend.

Uzuki Hirokawa

Pretty as long as she doesn't open her mouth, kind of a ditz if she does. Sweet Bullet's center singer. Nodoka talked her into attending college, but...

A ray of light pierced the clouds.

Like a ladder rolling down from above.

It lit the sea, the crowd…

…and the stage.

Rascal

DOES NOT DREAM of a Lost Singer

Hajime Kamoshida

Illustration by
Keji Mizoguchi

YEN ON

New York

Rascal Does Not Dream of a Lost Singer
Hajime Kamoshida

Translation by Andrew Cunningham
Cover art by Keji Mizoguchi

SEISHUN BUTA YARO WA MAYOERU SINGER NO YUME WO MINAI Vol. 10
©Hajime Kamoshida 2020
Edited by Dengeki Bunko
First published in Japan in 2020 by KADOKAWA CORPORATION, Tokyo. English
translation rights arranged with KADOKAWA CORPORATION, Tokyo through
TUTTLE-MORI AGENCY, INC., Tokyo.

English translation © 2023 by Yen Press, LLC

Yen On
150 West 30th Street, 19th Floor
New York, NY 10001

Visit us at yenpress.com
facebook.com/yenpress
twitter.com/yenpress
yenpress.tumblr.com
instagram.com/yenpress

First Yen On Edition: March 2023
Edited by Yen On Editorial: Ivan Liang
Designed by Yen Press Design: Andy Swist

Library of Congress Cataloging-in-Publication Data
Names: Kamoshida, Hajime, 1978– author. | Mizoguchi, Keji, illustrator.
Title: Rascal does not dream of bunny girl senpai / Hajime Kamoshida ;
illustration by Keji Mizoguchi.
Other titles: Seishun buta yarō. English
Description: New York, NY : Yen On, 2020. |
Contents: v. 1. Rascal does not dream of bunny girl senpai —
v. 2. Rascal does not dream of petite devil kohai —
v. 3. Rascal does not dream of logical witch —
v. 4. Rascal does not dream of siscon idol —
v. 5. Rascal does not dream of a sister home alone —
v. 6. Rascal does not dream of a dreaming girl —
v. 7. Rascal does not dream of his first love —
v. 8. Rascal does not dream of a sister venturing out —
v. 9. Rascal does not dream of a knapsack kid —
v. 10. Rascal does not dream of a lost singer
Identifiers: LCCN 2020004455 | ISBN 9781975399351 (v. 1 ; trade paperback) |
ISBN 9781975312541 (v. 2 ; trade paperback) | ISBN 9781975312565 (v. 3 ; trade paperback) |
ISBN 9781975312589 (v. 4 ; trade paperback) | ISBN 9781975312602 (v. 5 ; trade paperback) |
ISBN 9781975312626 (v. 6 ; trade paperback) | ISBN 9781975312640 (v. 7 ; trade paperback) |
ISBN 9781975312664 (v. 8 ; trade paperback) | ISBN 9781975312688 (v. 9 ; trade paperback) |
ISBN 9781975318512 (v. 10 ; trade paperback)
Subjects: CYAC: Fantasy.
Classification: LCC PZ7.1.K218 Ras 2020 | DDC [Fic]—dc23
LC record available at https://lccn.loc.gov/2020004455

ISBNs: 978-1-9753-1851-2 (paperback)
978-1-9753-1852-9 (ebook)

10 9 8 7 6 5 4 3 2 1

LSC-C

Printed in the United States of America

What defines me?
Does anyone know?
Voices echo in my ears
Breaking down the boundaries
I'm becoming one with everyone
And that's not good.

— From Touko Kirishima's "Social World"

Chapter
1
Adolescence Doesn't End

1

Sakuta Azusagawa wondered how much oolong tea it would take to justify the 1,200 yen it had cost him for the two-hour all-you-can-drink deal.

As he finished his third glass, he flagged a passing waitress and ordered another.

The rest of the table started piling on, ordering beers, highballs, lemon sours, and oolong-hais.

"I'll be right back!" she said with a smile. She vanished into the kitchen.

While they waited, Sakuta filled his mouth with the leftover ice. Before it melted, the waitress came back with a tray laden with glasses and mugs.

"Your oolong tea," she said, placing the glass in front of him. It had a straw sticking out of it, so he took a sip. It had the faint bitterness of oolong tea, no different from what they sold at the local grocery store.

A two-liter would cost him two hundred yen. The price of entry here would get him twelve whole liters.

Trying to drink that much in two hours was just torture. He'd live longer if he abandoned all hope of making it worth his while.

As these thoughts ran through his mind, a girl asked, "Mind if I sit here?"

He looked up to find her standing across the low table from him. She wore a long dress tied at the waist with a ribbonlike belt. On her shoulders was a military jacket with the sleeves rolled up.

Her hair was lightened just a tad, and half of it was pulled back in a loose knot—casual without looking clueless.

But her body was thin to the point of frail. She was smiling but didn't look all that confident—but maybe the teardrop mole just gave that impression.

"I'd rather you didn't," Sakuta admitted.

"……"

The teardrop girl held his gaze, blinking slowly. Like it had never occurred to her he might say no.

"Why is that?" she asked after a full three seconds.

She sat down across from him, brushing her skirt to keep it from wrinkling. Clearly, his attempted rebuff had been ineffective.

The girl put a half-finished drink down on the table. The ice was melting, and the sides were damp. She pulled over an appetizer plate, clearly settling in.

"I can feel the glares boring into my back already."

He didn't even need to turn around. She'd come from another table, leaving behind a short-haired female friend—and three men. When he'd ordered his tea, he'd spotted them with their phones out, pulling up contact info.

"They started sharing IDs, so I bailed."

His table was apparently a refuge.

"You could just refuse."

"Would that I could."

The teardrop girl seemed a bit at a loss, but that might just have been her default expression, so he couldn't tell if she actually *was*.

"You got a reason you can't?"

"…I just don't own a phone."

It took her a second to admit it.

"You're one of the few," he said.

"No one ever believes me."

The truth did not always sound true. Sometimes, it sounded like a bad lie. To make the truth convincing, she'd have to explain *why*, and she'd probably rather not.

"What, did you have a bad day and fling it into the ocean?"

"People actually do that?"

He had, but since she'd laughed, Sakuta elected not to volunteer that information.

"But how do you live without a phone?"

"Do people die without one?"

"So I'm told. The source is this high school girl I know."

"…A high school girl?"

That was definitely a note of contempt. Were college students not allowed to know anyone younger?

"A kohai at my old school," he tried to explain, before she reached any untoward conclusions.

"I guess that's kosher. Cheers."

The transition between those phrases was lost on him, but she held up a glass, and he tapped his to it. Each took a sip on their respective straws.

"Whatcha drinking?"

"Oolong tea."

"Me too."

"Yeah?"

"How many glasses to justify this tab?"

"Someone did the math. You'd need at least twelve liters."

"No one can drink that much."

"Pretty much what I thought."

Such a vapid conversation. They might legitimately be better off talking about the weather.

Keeping up the empty banter with a girl whose name he didn't even know seemed depressing, so Sakuta followed the spirit of the gathering and introduced himself.

"Sakuta Azusagawa, freshman. Statistical science major."

"Where'd that come from?" she chuckled, taking a bite of edamame. "These are good!" she muttered, then washed it down with tea.

The way she held the glass, the way she pinched her straw, even the way her lips wrapped round it—each gesture was weirdly feminine.

Sakuta could see why the boys had flocked to her. The regular dude inside him deemed her pretty cute. And he understood why they'd been eager to get her contact info.

That body language, plus the way the teardrop mole made her look permanently frazzled, stimulated the protective impulse. It was like she had a spell cast on her that made people fall in love at first sight.

"You watching me eat is pretty awkward," she said, glancing up at him. She didn't look the least bit put out, though. She was already on her next edamame.

"You know what this gathering is about?" Sakuta asked, glancing pointedly around the room.

They were inside an *izakaya* bar. Specifically, inside a room built for large parties, with tatami floors and dugouts beneath each table. Six tables in all, each seating four.

One table with just guys.

One table with just girls.

And four with a mix of genders—including the one the two of them were occupying.

They'd rented the room out. The twenty students here all went to the same college as Sakuta and were busy laughing, clapping, and pulling out their phones to exchange IDs.

It was the last day in September, Friday the thirtieth.

The new term had started that Monday, and everyone here was from the same class—a standard subject, part of the core curriculum, which was why students from a variety of majors were taking it. They'd be stuck together for the rest of the year, so they had planned a party to get to know one another better.

The bar itself was close to Yokohama Station. It was part of a chain and located in a shopping district a few minutes from the west exit. The all-you-can-drink ticket included, the price of admission had been 2,700 yen.

The mixer had now been going for a solid hour and a half, and everyone not at Sakuta's table was fairly buzzed. Their voices and laughter were getting louder and louder.

The party's organizers had planned for everyone to introduce themselves in due time, but everyone had long since forgotten that and wouldn't care if anyone brought it up. They were here for a good time.

"Miori Mitou, freshman. International management major."

"Thanks."

"Naturally, I knew you already."

"I'm kinda famous that way."

Or rather, his girlfriend was. Everyone in Japan knew and loved the famous actress Mai Sakurajima. She made movies, TV shows, commercials—even worked as a fashion model. If that weren't enough, she'd spent the back half of last year on a morning soap called *I'm Back*. Since Mai had first risen to stardom on a morning soap, it really *had* been a comeback. And had absolutely made her a household name again.

And their relationship had not stayed a rumor for long. It was quickly something everyone on campus knew for a fact.

Mai was also a student here, so there'd been no hiding it. Miori's *naturally* was only natural.

Six months after Sakuta enrolled, people had stopped bugging him about it. In fact, almost no one had ever asked him to his face if they were dating. He could count the number of times it had happened with his two hands.

He figured everyone was curious. But they also didn't want to act like a bunch of groupies. A regular vibe had developed on campus, like everyone was warning one another off.

"Must be nice dating someone pretty. I wish I was!"

"Mai's mine, and you can't have her."

"Jealous!"

That look went beyond envious into outright baleful.

"If you're looking to hook up, grab someone. Seems like you've got options."

He jerked his head at the table behind them. Another girl had joined in, and they were happily chattering away. But the volume in the room was high enough that he couldn't make anything out.

This time Miori really was glaring at him. "That's just mean," she said. "Why were you sitting all on your own anyway?"

"I didn't start that way."

"I know. I had a view from the other table."

Sakuta had been sitting with another dude from his major, Takumi Fukuyama. That guy had moved to another table a while back, having spent the first hour looping through the same unproductive conversation.

"I want a girlfriend!"

"Then go talk to a girl."

"Too awkward."

"Then I'll talk to one."

"I'll come with!"

"Go on ahead."

"I can't!"

Eventually, Sakuta had gone to the bathroom and come back to find him sitting at one of the girls' tables. A tribute to the power of alcohol. It had even scored him some contact info.

He relayed this to Miori, who took a bite out of a chicken nugget and said, "You could have moved to another table, too."

She didn't look like a girl who ate such high-calorie food a lot, but she was really savoring it. There was a look of bliss on her face. She swallowed, and her chopsticks reached for another. There'd been four on the plate to start with—the idea being to split the plate among the four people at the table. Since only the two of them were sitting here, this was still her share. But given the total number of occupants in the room, it was depriving *someone* of chicken.

But even as he crunched those numbers, Miori helped herself to a third nugget, clearly staking a claim to the whole plate.

"Azusagawa, why are you even here?"

"Mostly the food." He reached out his chopsticks and grabbed the last nugget before she could. "The other tables have too many people, so there's less food to go around."

Sakuta hadn't planned to come at all, but Takumi had been so insistent, he'd given in.

"Everyone's starving," Miori said, glancing around. She was clearly referring to the desperation driving their social interactions.

"You're different, then?"

College wasn't like high school. No one had an assigned classroom. No single place where everybody met on a daily basis. No designated seating. All classes were held in various places, and people grabbed seats as they came in.

The biggest change was that you no longer really had "classmates."

If you shared a major, you also shared a list of required classes and were more likely to run into the same crowd there. But the bulk of the freshman year was taken up by core curriculum stuff, and less than half the classes he was taking were major specific. There was not much pressure to connect to those around you—at least, there was a lot less than in high school classrooms.

There, all relationships were defined by that room. And Sakuta was finally free of that stifling oppression.

Liberty abounded.

But that also meant newcomers to college were not guaranteed a natural home.

Which was why people who happened to be in the same class were voluntarily gathering, forming makeshift communities, and trying to create their own home ground. Hungry for good times and social ties. Or maybe just saying a prayer in the hopes that they might leave here with a new girlfriend or boyfriend.

"I'm pretty famished myself," Miori said, polishing off that third nugget.

She chewed away, eyes on the party around her, but despite what she said, she didn't seem to be after anything in particular. This was simply a passing opportunity to watch them all whoop it up from a distance. Her gaze neither warm nor scornful.

Miori might not even care if she was starving or not. He didn't think she even intended her words to carry much meaning. It was like they were just filling space.

"Uh, so only five minutes left," the dude who'd set this up said, using his hands as a megaphone. "Let's start wrapping up. After-party's karaoke, so please do come."

Only half the crowd even heard him.

"There's an after-party. Azusagawa, you going?"

"Nope. Got work after this."

"This late? You work nights?"

It wasn't really late enough to call night. It had only just turned six. The party had started as the *izakaya* opened, at four—pretty early for drunken revelry.

"Doing private tutoring for a cram school today."

"Today?"

"I also wait tables at a restaurant."

Sakuta finished off his tea. The last drops spluttered against his straw.

"Teaching junior high?"

"First-year high school," he said, picking up his backpack.

"Showing high school girls all the tricks. Naughty."

"I'm teaching 'em *math* tricks, and I've got male students, too."

At the moment, he was actually only teaching two students—one boy, one girl. Since the students picked their teachers, his pool would increase only if someone chose him. His student quantity and classes taught directly affected how much he made, so he certainly would like a few more, but that was clearly gonna require patience.

The party was still going strong, but he slipped out, putting his shoes on first. Out of the corner of his eye, he saw Miori tying the laces on her sneakers.

"No after-party?"

"Can't stand karaoke."

She made that face again, but this time it seemed genuine. Maybe it wasn't. He didn't know her well enough to be sure.

"Let's go before anyone spots us," Miori said, glancing back at the hall. "It'll be a pain if anyone tries to drag us along," she added, winking at him. Then she led him out of the bar.

Outside, they were hit with a wave of humidity. September was on the way out the door, but these days, summers just didn't wanna leave.

It being a Friday, there were huge throngs pouring out of the station into the shopping district.

Likely bound for dates, mixers, and parties.

Pushing against the tide, Sakuta and Miori crossed the bridge over the Katabira River, then followed the bank to avoid the crowds. Miori wasn't a fast walker and sometimes had to trot to catch up, but she never yelled at him for walking too fast.

Sakuta slowed his pace a bit anyway, glancing at her over his shoulder.

"You kinda ditched your friend."

"Manami?"

"I dunno her name."

"I'm good. If I'd stayed longer, she'd have been pissed."

Miori caught up with him and sighed.

"Ah…don't want the boys your friend likes coming after *you*, right?"

She probably hadn't expected him to understand, and judging by her vague answer, she never intended to explain further. That explained her somewhat awkward smile.

"Very perceptive," she managed.

There was genuine surprise in her glance.

"Knew a high school girl in similar circumstances."

She'd been asked out by a friend's crush, and it had not gone well.

"You know too many high school girls."

Miori took a step away from him, her tone suddenly guarded.

"Don't worry, it's the same one."

And she'd be in college in another six months.

"Let's say I believe you."

"Scout's honor."

"Taking the JR, Azusagawa?"

The conversation changed without the waters clearing. If he dug his heels in, that would probably just dig him into a hole, so he let the sudden segue pass without comment.

"Tokaido Line to Fujisawa. You?"

"To Ofuna."

She sounded pleased with herself, likely because it was one station closer. And closer to Yokohama Station meant closer to the Keikyu Line they took to college.

Their school was at Kanazawa-hakkei Station.

"You grow up there?" he asked, pretty sure she hadn't. Miori didn't seem like the Ofuna type. It was a city-run university, so most students came from Yokohama or at least this prefecture. Those who came from out of town had a different air about them somehow.

"Nope, moved there on my own after getting in."

"Then you could have picked somewhere closer."

"It's close to Kamakura."

Sakuta had obviously meant closer to college, but the answer he got was certainly distinctive. To be fair, Kamakura was nice. He'd taken Mai there a few times.

"You're from Fujisawa?"

"Feels like I am."

He'd been living there for three years now, so he no longer felt like an outsider. The Yokohama suburb where he'd actually grown up would feel far stranger. He hadn't been back since junior high graduation.

They reached the main drag and got stuck at the first light.

"Oh, right," Miori said, pulling a little plastic case out of her tote bag. It rattled when shaken—filled with little mints. From the sound, it was still full.

She popped three at once into her mouth and handed the entire box to Sakuta.

"Does my breath smell *that* bad?"

"There was garlic in that chicken coating. And you're teaching in a bit, right?"

"Yeah, sure, thanks."

Sakuta popped three mints himself. His mouth grew frosty. The chill reached his nostrils.

"Not saying this in lieu of thanks…"

"Hmm?" she asked, giving him the side-eye.

"Careful what guys you do that to."

"Why?"

"I mean, it seems like you *don't* want them hanging all over you."

"Then we're safe. It's only you here."

"Am I being targeted?"

"I'm being relaxed. I mean, you aren't ever gonna fall for *me*. You've got the cutest girlfriend in Japan."

"The world, but otherwise true."

This made Miori laugh out loud. "You *would* say that," she said with a giggle.

The light still wasn't changing.

"……"

"……"

As their conversation trailed off, both found themselves looking at the same thing. Across the street, a woman in a suit was handing out pocket tissues. She was in her early twenties. She'd taken her jacket off, but she must have been out here for a while, because her shirt was drenched with sweat. Her bangs were plastered to her forehead. She was likely a new hire, joining whichever company earlier that year.

She was handing out tissues with staunch dedication, but no one was taking any.

Everyone kept sailing right past her.

"Azusagawa, you ever worked a job like that?"

"I have not."

"Nobody takes the tissues."

"Nope."

"Maybe only the two of us can see her."

Miori dropped that bombshell without changing her tone of voice at all.

"No way."

"What, you've never heard of Adolescence Syndrome?"

"......"

When had he last heard that phrase? Long enough that he didn't react right away.

"People can't see you, you can see the future, there are two of you—all kinds of symptoms."

"Huh."

"You didn't hear stories about it at school?"

The light turned green.

"Stories, sure." Sakuta moved out first, and Miori lagged a step behind. "But they're just stories."

Across the street, he took a tissue packet from the woman.

"Thank you," she said. The tissues came with an ad for newly constructed condos. Sakuta didn't think he looked like he could afford one. Maybe this lady was getting tissue tunnel vision and had forgotten what she was actually advertising.

As these thoughts ran through his head, another man walked by and took a tissue. He was in his fifties, definitely more her target demo.

Quite a few people were taking tissues now.

"Looks like it's not just us."

"What do you know," Miori lamented.

"And that lady's hardly the syndrome age bracket."

She was clearly in her twenties.

"Does adolescence have a hard limit?"

"I wouldn't know."

It probably varied by the individual. There were no clear defini-
tions. It wasn't like everyone automatically became a grown-up the
moment they turned twenty.

"Are you still an adolescent, Azusagawa?"

"I'd prefer to think I'm past all that."

"You are in college now."

"Are you free of it?"

"I think…it's still got me."

"Any particular reason?"

"I mean, I've yet to land a boyfriend."

"Ah, I see."

"Wow, you're totally giving me that smug 'already taken' look."

Miori shot him a frosty glare. Then she swiped the pack of tissues
from him and started walking in the direction of the underground
entrance.

"The gates are the other way."

She'd been moving toward the stairs to the Yokohama Station
underground mall.

"I've got shopping to do first. See you around."

She fluttered a hand at him and disappeared below without looking
back.

"Hmm."

He wasn't sure what to make of Miori Mitou. She was friendly and
expressive, but it was like there was a line between them, and she would
come no closer. She'd probably split up here because they'd otherwise end up sharing a train. Maybe he was overthinking it, but she
seemed like the type who'd try to avoid that.

She'd taken the tissues (which were useful) and left him with the
condo ad (which was not), so he shoved that in his backpack and
headed into the station proper.

As he passed through the JR gates, he found himself wondering just
how long it had been since he'd heard anyone mention Adolescence
Syndrome.

2

At Yokohama Station, he hopped on the Tokaido Line. The train was packed with business types and students, all headed home. But since it was Friday and people had things to do, it was less packed than usual.

Sakuta secured a position leaning against the door between cars and took out the textbook he was tutoring with. He flipped to page 25 and scanned the example quadratic function, reviewing the material before he had to teach it.

As he did, the train moved steadily along, passing through the shopping distract around Yokohama Station and out into the residential areas beyond. As a station approached, the buildings grew taller, and once past the station, those gave way to quiet neighborhoods. Back and forth the scenery went.

When he'd first started this commute, he'd missed the sea and sky and horizon, but after six months of it, he'd learned how to make the most of this time. Generally he spent it like this, prepping for his classes.

But today he couldn't focus.

He knew exactly why.

The words Miori Mitou had said after the party.

——*"You've never heard of Adolescence Syndrome?"*

When was the last time he'd heard anyone say that?

Certainly not since he'd started college. And before that...well, he'd spent his third year of high school with his nose firmly buried in a book, prepping for entrance exams, and hadn't heard much of anything.

That meant it had been at least a year and a half.

Realizing others could no longer perceive you.

Living out a projection of the future.

Splitting into two versions of yourself.

Swapping bodies with someone else.

The pain in your heart physically manifesting and affecting your body.

Traveling to the future.

Fleeing into a potential world.

Sakuta had encountered all these types of Adolescence Syndrome.

But for the last year and a half, nothing had happened.

That was a good thing, so he hadn't been worried about it or counted the days.

Before he realized it, all this time had passed.

The Tokaido Line train stopped at Totsuka and Ofuna before arriving at Fujisawa Station right on schedule.

Sakuta joined the line of people filing through the gates and emerged at the station's north exit. He turned left at the electronics store and saw the sign for the cram school he worked at up ahead. It was on the fifth floor of an office building.

He took the elevator up and, despite the hour, said "Good morning" to the front desk staff.

Unlike regular school offices, there were no doors or walls here— the whole floor was visible.

There was an open space for students with several tables in it, and the only thing dividing that from the staff room was a waist-high counter. It was a setup designed so students would have easy access to the teaching staff.

Even now, there was a student at the counter, asking a teacher about their English essay.

"Morning, Azusagawa. Make it a good one."

This came from the school's principal, a man in his midforties. From the way he was nervously keeping an eye on the phone, something must have gone wrong.

Sakuta wanted no part of that, so he simply bobbed his head and moved to the locker room.

He opened the locker with his name on it and took out a garment that looked like someone had combined a white lab coat and a suit jacket, then split the difference. This was the teachers' uniform here, worn over their regular clothes.

He took the textbook out of his backpack, dumped some more mints in his mouth (just in case), and left the locker room.

He headed for the the row of classrooms in the rear of the main area.

Despite being called "rooms," these were just little study cubicles, maybe eight feet by six feet each. The entrances had no doors, and the walls didn't reach the ceiling. If you listened closely, it wasn't hard to hear people talking in the next cubicle over.

There were two students waiting for him, one boy and one girl. They were seated across the central aisle from each other. The girl was sitting quietly, but the boy's attention was on his phone. Since he had headphones on, he was likely playing a rhythm game.

"Let's begin."

"Okay."

Only the girl answered. She already had her book open to page 25.

Her name was Juri Yoshiwa.

She sported a healthy tan but had a quiet, unflappable disposition. She was on her school's beach volleyball team and was attending this school to keep her grades up. She wore the uniform of Minegahara—the high school Sakuta himself had attended. She was five foot three, on the short side for her sport of choice.

Most junior athletes Sakuta had met were Mai's height or taller. This girl might only be in her first year of high school, but most girls stopped growing around then.

The boy muttered "'Sup" but failed to look up from his phone. He just kept tapping away at his game.

His name was Kenta Yamada.

Like Juri, he was a first-year at Minegahara. But they were in different classes and didn't really know each other there.

In his case, his first-term grades had been so bad, he'd started coming here in summer to improve his baseline knowledge...and he'd spent a chunk of the first class grumbling about how his parents had made him come.

He was five foot five but looked taller because his hair was spiky. He hadn't mentioned sports at all, but from his build, he'd probably been on a team in junior high.

"Yamada, we're starting."

The clock showed exactly seven PM, and class was in session.

"Just two more seconds!"

"One. Two. Page twenty-five, quadratic functions."

"Argh, Sakuta-sensei! You made me blow a perfect run!"

Ignoring Kenta's moaning, Sakuta started explaining how to use the functions. This had been on the first test after summer vacation ended, and they'd both missed it. He took the example and worked through the solution on the whiteboard. Once that was done, he had them each solve a practice question that followed the same pattern as the example. He was ready to help each individually as they got stuck.

Juri did as she was told, working through the problem in her book.

Kenta frowned, thinking—and then gave up.

"Sakuta-sensei!" he said, slumping down on the desk.

"What?"

"I don't get it."

"What don't you get?"

"How to get a cute girlfriend."

Not the answer he'd expected.

"Focus on classroom problems."

"You've got the world's cutest girlfriend—you must have tips!"

"I might have the universe's cutest girlfriend, but I can't teach you that."

This was not the first time Kenta had brought this subject up.

"I only picked your class because I thought you'd have insider knowledge to share! Augh, I should have gone with Futaba-sensei instead. At least she's got big tits!"

The "Futaba-sensei" he'd mentioned was Rio Futaba, a friend of

Sakuta's from high school. She was now attending a national science university and had started tutoring here a month before he had.

"I'd start by remembering that girls hate it when guys say stuff like that."

He glanced at Juri, but she was grimly working her way through the problem.

"So keep it to myself?"

"I think you learned about freedom of thought in social studies."

"Freedom to be lewd!"

Sakuta had no clue how he'd reached *that* conclusion, but it wasn't necessarily wrong.

"I get wanting a girlfriend in general, but do you even have someone in mind?"

The class was clearly not getting anywhere otherwise, so Sakuta played along.

"I'm game for any girls, so long as they're cute."

That answer was downright refreshingly dumb.

"I think what's inside counts, too. Might not be convincing when I say it, I realize."

"I like big boobs, too."

"By *inside*, I meant personality."

Not what they had inside their clothes.

"Azusagawa-sensei."

Juri finally voiced an objection. He glanced down at her page, and she'd solved a single problem and stopped. It must have been hard to focus with this conversation happening next to her.

"Best we got back on topic."

"Then tell me how to get a girlfriend!"

"Nothing but math here."

"Whyyy?!"

"Because that's what I'm paid for."

"I can't focus if I don't have a girlfriend!"

"Yamada, why are you so desperate?"

"I mean, if you've got a girl, you can have sex all the time!"

"……"

Sakuta figured this was what Yamada had been getting at, but hearing it out loud still left him speechless.

"……What, is that wrong?"

"As long as you think that, you'll never get a girlfriend."

Even if he was a student, that would just earn him pity. Kenta hadn't noticed, but Juri was giving him a look of frosty contempt.

At this point, there was a knock—since there was no door, someone had rapped on the cubicle wall.

"Azusagawa-sensei."

He turned around and found Rio Futaba in the entrance. Since she worked here, too, she had on the same uniform.

"Got a moment?"

She was acting distant and was clearly annoyed.

"What?"

"Out here."

Her glance ordered him out of the room.

"Solve those problems," he said, and he left Kenta and Juri to it, exiting the cubicle.

Rio led him over toward the free space and sighed the moment she stopped moving.

"Keep your classes focused. We're getting complaints from the neighboring cubicle."

She glanced at the cubicle next to his, where she'd been teaching physics.

"I'm taking things seriously."

"The words we're hearing suggest otherwise."

There was little doubt that meant *boobs* and *sex*.

"I didn't say them."

If he glanced down to see how taut her shirtfront was, there was no telling what she'd say, so he diligently avoided that.

Rio sighed dramatically. Again.

"Try not to get yourself fired, too."

"Too?"

Like someone else had.

"Look."

Rio glanced at the free area outside the staff office. A young male teacher was busy pleading with the principal.

"It's not true! I swear!"

"Calm down. We'll talk in my office."

"This is all a big misunderstanding! Right?"

The teacher turned to look at a female student standing a good three yards away. She was also wearing a Minegahara uniform and had a female teacher with her. Her head was down, and she looked plagued by guilt.

"I'm sorry. I never thought of you that way."

What did she mean by that? He didn't have to ask. The awkward tension made it all too clear what had gone down here.

Teacher-student romantic complications. Judging by the student's comment, she'd never intended to start anything like that.

So likely the male teacher had seen signals where none existed and made a pass at her.

"You said you rely on me! That you wanted my help with stuff outside of school!"

On his way here, Miori had cracked a joke about this exact situation.

——*"Showing high school girls all the tricks. Naughty."*

But seeing it actually happen for real hit different.

"I'm sorry," she said, striking down his pleas, though doing so seemed to pain her.

"No…," he whispered, staggering.

"This way," the principal said. "We'll talk this through."

"…Right."

The principal put a hand on his back and pushed him away, like he was a captured criminal. But he looked less like a man who repented his misdeeds than a spurned suitor.

They vanished into the office.

"Um, what's gonna happen to him?" the girl asked, concern written on her face.

"Don't you worry about it," the female teacher said.

It was obvious there were certain steps they'd have to take. Given what he'd done, that was unavoidable.

"Don't be too hard on him. I'm really okay."

"I'll let the principal know. For now, you'd better go home."

"...Yeah," the girl said.

But she didn't move, clearly still worried about what consequences the teacher would face. Her eyes never left the office door. Sakuta had a better view now, and she looked like a straight-A student, the kind of girl who was nice to everyone. Her hair was done conservatively, and her uniform was impeccable. What little makeup she wore was natural-style. In high school, he'd definitely have mistaken that for no makeup at all.

"Don't end up like him, Azusagawa."

"Do I look like I'd go for a student?"

"No, but..."

"See?"

"But what about the other way around?"

"I'm more popular than you'd think."

"Yes, that's why I'm warning you."

"...Uh, Futaba."

"What?"

"You're supposed to deny that. I was joking."

"But you *are* more popular than you'd think."

Rio's tone made it clear this was a statement of fact, and he couldn't argue with that.

"Then we'll just have to hope having the cutest girlfriend in the universe keeps me safe."

"Didn't you say you hadn't even seen Sakurajima for, like, a month now?"

Mai was in Hokkaido, filming a movie. College summer vacation ran for nearly all of August and September, so she'd filled that with two starring roles.

The first had wrapped in August, and she'd come back from Niigata with *sasa dango*. She'd called the other night to tell him the second would take her till the start of next week.

"Don't worry, she'll make up for it."

"Then I'll get back to class."

"No time for my corny bragging?"

"Just keep them on task."

With that, Rio headed back to her class, and Kenta poked his head out of the cubicle.

"Sakuta-sensei, are you done yet?"

"Yeah, I got yelled at 'cause of you."

"Whaaat?"

He really didn't seem to get why. But then he blinked, looking over Sakuta's shoulder.

"……"

Kenta said nothing, but he was obviously looking at the girl from before. She was still lingering in the free space.

"You know her?" Sakuta asked.

"Sara Himeji. She's in my class," he said.

"Hmm."

He knew *both* her names. Interesting.

"What?"

"That your type?"

"?!"

Sakuta had been talking off the cuff, but that had apparently touched a nerve.

"No!" Kenta said, clearly irate.

"Cool."

"C'mon, Sakuta-sensei! Teach!"

"Well, I'm glad to see you motivated."

If Kenta tried to derail class again, he might have to bring this back up.

As it was, the rest of the class stayed focused. Rio didn't have to yell at him twice.

3

When class wrapped up and Sakuta left the cram school, it was almost nine. The class itself lasted eighty minutes, and the rest of that time had been logging reports on the students' level of understanding and waiting for Rio.

Outside, he walked with her toward the station.

"Oh, right," Rio said, like she'd just remembered something.

"Mm?"

"I got a text from Kunimi earlier."

"What'd he say?"

"He successfully completed firefighter training."

"Oh, was that today?"

Yuuma Kunimi had taken the local civil servant exam right after graduation. It was a fire department requirement.

He'd cleared that hurdle readily enough, but they weren't about to take an ordinary high school student and dispatch them right away when lives were at stake.

Yuuma was first sent to a training center, where he'd spent six months living and breathing their training regimen. This info had come with the exam results.

He'd been there since April.

The last day of September was the six-month mark exactly.

"And he said he'd already locked a posting, so we shouldn't worry."

"Why would anyone ever worry about Kunimi?"

Yuuma always came through.

Sakuta's line got a bit of a smile out of Rio; she likely agreed with the sentiment.

"He's starting Monday, so once he settles in, he'd like to meet up for tea."

"As long as he's paying."

"I figured you'd say that, so I already told him as much."

By this point, they'd reached Fujisawa Station.

Rio lived in Hon-Kugenuma, a stop down the Odakyu Enoshima Line. They split up with a simple good-bye.

This late, the air was finally starting to feel like fall. Enjoying the chill, Sakuta walked home from the station alone.

He crossed the Sakai River bridge and started up a long, gentle slope. There was a little garden along the way, and a while after that, he saw the apartment building up ahead. The place they'd moved into when he started high school.

Once he'd made sure the mailbox was empty, he found an elevator waiting on the first floor. He got in and pressed the button for the fifth floor.

He'd considered moving for college. Of course, he only considered places he could actually afford on his paltry earnings.

Ultimately, that hadn't happened. He'd had good reason to stay put.

On the fifth floor, he left the elevator and headed all the way left to his apartment door.

Insert key and open.

"I'm back, Nasuno."

He called out to his cat as he came in.

Something felt out of place.

There were two pairs of shoes that hadn't been here when he left.

"Oh, hey, Sakuta. Welcome home."

Slippers flapping, Mai came out to meet him.

"Thanks. Nice to have you back, Mai."

"Nice to *be* back."

"I thought your shoot was supposed to take a few more days?"

"The rest we can do on set, so I came home."

It had been a full month since he saw Mai's smile in person.

"......"

"Why are you staring?"

"I feel like you've become even more beautiful."

"Isn't it nice?"

With that, she turned and headed back into the living room. Sakuta followed.

"Oh, there you are," Kaede said. His sister was sprawled out on the living room couch, Nasuno clutched in her arms. She was playing with the cat as she watched a game show on TV.

It didn't air at this hour, so she must have recorded it. He saw familiar faces on-screen—Nodoka and Uzuki. The latter's daffy comments had the MC and other contestants in stitches.

"You're back, Kaede?"

He'd recognized her shoes at the entrance.

Sakuta lived here in Fujisawa, and their parents lived in Yokohama. Kaede was rotating between the two domiciles, splitting her time evenly between them both. She was a high school student but attended a remote-learning school, which meant she was free to live where she pleased. You could take classes anywhere, as long as you owned a phone.

"I told you I had a shift today," she said, glaring at the answering machine. The light on it was definitely flashing.

She'd started working in the spring—the same restaurant he worked at. That had been what Kaede wanted and was a major factor in why they hadn't moved. In return, part of the rent was now coming out of her wages.

"Seriously, Sakuta—you've *got* to buy a phone."

"I never dreamed I'd hear those words from you, Kaede."

He'd been shocked enough when she'd wanted one of her own. She'd been badly hurt by classmates in junior high, and phone-based social problems had been a big part of that.

"Mai, you'd rather Sakuta owned a phone, too, right?"

"Yes, but I'm used to it now."

"You can't just let Mai indulge your bullshit."

She'd failed to secure Mai's support, so she immediately went back on the offensive.

"I'll think about it if I have wages left over."

"That's what you always say. Whatever!"

Dropping the issue, she peeled herself off the couch and deposited Nasuno on the floor.

"You're not ready for a bath yet? I'll go first, then."

She paused the video and headed toward the bathroom.

"What, you hadn't already?"

"I was waiting for you to get home first."

"That's sweet."

The door slammed behind her.

This was probably her way of giving him time to talk to Mai alone. He couldn't decide if that was how considerate high school girls should be or just his sister trying to act all mature.

"You eat yet?"

"I'm good: I ate at a class party before work."

"Fall for any cute girls there?"

On the phone last night, he'd told her his core curriculum class was holding a gathering. Not only had she not objected, she'd suggested it was a good opportunity to meet more people. But she had wrapped it up with a final threat not to even consider cheating on her.

"I did not."

"Shame."

"Oh, but..."

"But what? Why is there a but?"

"There was this one girl."

"Oh?"

"She's in college but doesn't own a phone."

"...Is the punch line gonna be that only you can see her?"

He understood why she'd react that way. It was just that weird. Every college student had a phone these days. She was certainly the first phoneless college student Sakuta had met. Besides himself anyway.

"You've made me nervous," he said. "I'll have to verify that on Monday."

"You do that. Well, I'd better get going."

Mai grabbed her suitcase off the couch.

"Already?"

"Got an early start tomorrow. I'll be back on campus Wednesday."

She was already moving to the door.

"I'll walk you down."

He took a step, but she grabbed his arm.

"Don't want anyone taking photos, so this is far enough. The office is on my case about it."

She used him for balance as she did up the ankle straps on her pumps.

"I left a present in the fridge. Share it with Kaede."

"I'd better eat my half before she devours it all."

Mai laughed, then cupped his cheeks in her hands.

"What?" he asked, making octopus lips.

"Nothing," she said, giggling.

Probably just a bit giddy about seeing him again.

And that made her feel mischievous.

That was all.

And if Mai was having fun, that was all he needed.

No matter how trivial the reason, Mai's smile was enough for him.

She let go of his cheeks, fluttered her fingers, said "Bye," and was out the door.

Sakuta savored the lingering embers of her mirth and quietly locked the door behind her.

4

The weekend passed, and Monday arrived.

October 3 was a rainy morning.

His classes that day started from second period, at 10:30 AM. He took his time getting up and getting ready to leave. "Take care," Kaede said, seeing him out the door at 9:15.

The temperatures were getting a bit more autumny, but the humidity still spoke to summer. In a T-shirt and easy pants (cropped to leave his ankles bare), he was pretty comfortable.

This summer just wouldn't go away. When it did end, it would probably lead directly into a sudden winter. It felt like fall was getting shorter and shorter, or was that just him?

With those thoughts running through his mind, he reached Fujisawa Station. There were still lingering traces of the morning rush. No uniformed students left, but plenty of older students and business suits.

On the station's second floor, he went through the JR gates and down to the Tokaido Line platform. He didn't have to wait long before the 9:32 to Koganei came in.

The usual train, the usual ride—it took about twenty minutes.

Sakuta got off at Yokohama Station and switched to the Keikyu Line's distinctive red cars. Kanagawa Prefecture was shaped like a dog, and this express went all the way to the front legs at Misakiguchi. And there was no extra charge for riding the express—you could just use a regular ticket.

He got on near the front of the train, avoiding the congestion.

As the train pulled out, he stood near the door, watching the scenery go by. When he'd first started college, the view alone had not been enough for him to place himself, but after six months, he had a much better grasp on things. He'd naturally acquired the gist of what buildings and offices were where.

After riding for a while, he passed a high school known for having one of the best baseball teams in the prefecture. That was a sign they were almost at his station.

Since he still had a little time to kill, Sakuta let his eyes run across the interior ads. He found one for a fashion magazine with Mai on the cover. Two college-looking girls were talking about it. "That outfit's so cute!" "It's cute because Mai Sakurajima is wearing it." "Point taken." Et cetera, et cetera.

"She's even cuter in person."

"The world is so not fair."

Sounded like they'd seen her out and about. If they were on this train at this hour, odds were high they went to Sakuta's university. Which meant odds were high they knew who he was, too.

If he kept staring, they'd catch him looking, so he turned away. And found himself looking right at someone *he* knew.

Ikumi Akagi was standing in front of the next door down. One shoulder was resting against the door itself, but she kept her back bolt upright. She was holding a thick book in both hands, and there was no Japanese on the cover. He suspected the contents were entirely in English. She was very focused.

She'd been his classmate back in junior high.

Three years later, they'd run into each other at college.

But they hadn't spoken since that encounter.

——*"You're Azusagawa, right?"*

——*"Akagi?"*

——*"Yeah. Been a while."*

That had been the end of it. Nodoka had caught up with him a moment later, and Ikumi had promptly said "Bye" and left. She hadn't spoken to him since. He'd seen her around on campus but hadn't felt compelled to make contact.

They hadn't known each other well, even back in the day. She was just one of thirty classmates. The kind of person whose name you forget the moment you graduate.

Reuniting after a three-year gap had provoked no real emotions, and the encounter had led to nothing of note.

That probably was true for Ikumi, too. She'd just spotted a familiar face at orientation and said hello. Nothing more to it.

The only real development made over the last six months was that he'd learned she was in the nursing program.

Sakuta's university had a medical school, and anyone trying to become a nurse would be in Ikumi's division. The medical school had its own dedicated campus, but since the bulk of the first year was devoted to the core curriculum, first-years from other schools were also centered on the Kanazawa-hakkei campus. Ikumi was one of these.

At the party last week, two guys from the nursing school had come, plus one girl from the main school of medicine.

She must have sensed eyes on her. Ikumi's head turned his way. He was pretty sure she'd worn glasses before but wasn't now. But her gaze clearly focused on him. She blinked twice. Her expression was exactly as it had been when she was reading. She blinked a third time, then went back to her original stance. One shoulder against the door, glancing briefly outside to confirm the rain had stopped.

The train reached Kanazawa-hakkei Station without anything else transpiring between the two of them.

On the platform, Sakuta headed up the stairs to the gates. Kanazawa-hakkei Station had recently finished a major remodel, and the area around the gate still looked very new.

The Seaside Line station had originally been a short distance away, but the remodel had moved it into the station, allowing for smooth transfers.

The easiest way to campus was to go up the stairs and over to the west side of the station. The bridge over the tracks was nice and wide.

Once down the stairs, it was a three-minute walk along the tracks to campus. There weren't that many students on the road with him today. The college itself had five times the students his high school had had, but since the class start times were all over the map, the station was never as packed in the morning.

The students coming in now all started with second period.

Sakuta joined the flow of the crowd through the front gate. There, he was greeted by two rows of gingko trees running right down the middle of the campus.

When he'd first come here to sit the exam, he'd looked at these trees and thought it made the place feel like a real college campus. This sort of scenery popped up a lot in college-set movies or TV shows.

To the left inside the gate was the main gym, where the orientation had been. Beyond that was the sports field. Five or six students were doing some running there. Likely soccer team members getting some extra training in between classes. The teams seemed to have a lot more control over their schedules than high school teams had.

Across the gingko trees from the field was a three-story building where the majority of the actual classes were held. It looked like a giant square, but it was actually a box with a park in the center. His second-period class was in there.

Near the center of the grounds was a noteworthy clock—the university symbol—and he turned right just in front of that.

Sakuta heard footsteps running up behind him, and a moment later, someone slapped his back.

"Azusagawa, 'sup!"

"Hey there, Fukuyama."

Takumi Fukuyama started walking with him. He was the first person Sakuta had seriously spoken to after enrolling. He'd also been the first to work up the courage to ask, "It true you're going out with Mai Sakurajima?" And since their elective choices had lined up a lot, they'd wound up spending practically all their time together.

"How'd it go Friday?" Takumi asked, his curiosity very apparent.

"How'd what go?"

Sakuta genuinely wasn't sure why he was asking.

"You earned the enmity of every dude there! You took Mitou home with you!"

"I did no such thing."

"You left at the same time!"

"Yeah, when the party ended. I had to go to work, so we split up at the station."

"That's so boring. Course, if anything had happened, I would've held it against you."

There were no right answers here.

As Takumi nattered on, they went inside and headed for the third floor one stair at a time.

Takumi was telling him all about who'd sung what at karaoke, who'd been any good, and how popular Touko Kirishima's songs had been.

"She's still pretty big, then, huh?"

He'd heard the name before. Touko Kirishima had gotten her start online and was massively popular with the teen-to-early-twenties demographic. She'd never once shown her face in public, fueling endless speculations about who she really was. All they really knew was her gender and that she was roughly the same age as her audience.

"More like she's big *now* or maybe will be."

Sakuta wasn't sure what that meant, but clearly she wasn't going anywhere. Sakuta had no idea online singers could get their songs in karaoke machines.

"I mean, look."

Takumi held out his phone.

It showed a pair of bare feet standing on the grass. Delicate looking, probably a girl's. As he watched, beautiful, powerful a capella vocals started playing.

The camera angle changed, showing her from behind. More scenery was revealed—she was standing in the center of a stadium. No one was in the stands. The shape of the roof suggested it was probably the International Stadium Yokohama.

The next shot was from the side, showing only her mouth as she hit the chorus.

All the angles were pretty extreme, never revealing the whole girl. It never showed her face above the lips. She looked a little familiar, but the song ended before he could figure out why.

The last shot was of her ears, revealing that this had been a commercial for wireless headphones.

"That's a Touko Kirishima song," Takumi said.

"So…was that *her*?"

"Apparently not."

"Huh?"

"That was a mysterious commercial beauty who can really sing."

How could he call her a beauty when you couldn't see her face? Okay, so she had given off that vibe.

"It's a cover, basically."

"So who's the girl in the commercial?"

Keeping her face hidden like that got him interested.

"I'm telling you, it's a mystery."

"Nobody knows?"

"Yep."

What a headache. Touko Kirishima was a mystery online singer. And the girl covering her song in the commercial was also unidentified.

"But there are rumors it's Mai Sakurajima."

"If it was Mai, they'd be better off showing her face."

She'd been working since early childhood, and with her return to the morning soaps, people from all walks of life knew who she was. And if that was Mai, there was no way Sakuta wouldn't have realized it. Even if he could only see her feet, back, and lips.

"No, not *her*—they say Touko Kirishima is actually Mai Sakurajima."

That was news to Sakuta.

"Lots of people pushing that theory," Takumi said, scrolling on his phone to pull something up.

"Watch your feet."

It would be bad to stand idly by while someone fell down the stairs 'cause they were too busy with their phone.

"Is that a pickup line?" Takumi laughed.

Sakuta pretended he hadn't heard this.

"What do you make of it? Is Mai Sakurajima actually Touko Kirishima?"

"No way in hell."

At the very least, Mai hadn't told him anything about that. And she was the one who'd first told him about Touko Kirishima. A younger colleague from her agency had insisted she was the next big thing, so Mai had tried her music out.

"The voice *is* kinda similar, though."

At that point, they reached room 301. Today's subject was foreign languages. Sakuta had gone with Spanish as his elective.

"Later."

"Yep."

Takumi had picked Chinese—on the grounds that he knew some kanji—so they split up in the hall, and Sakuta headed into class alone.

In the classroom, the first thing he heard was loud laughter. The source was five girls clustered near the doorway. They were all wearing long skirts somewhere between yellow and khaki, plus matching T-shirts, and sneakers. Their outfits were so similar you could tell people they were an idol group in costume, and he'd believe it.

Sakuta wasn't really one to criticize fashion. Takumi had also been wearing a T-shirt, easy pants, and a black backpack, so they'd pretty much matched, too. Sakuta's style was what Mai had given him to celebrate passing the entrance exam.

He slipped past the chatty girls and grabbed a seat on the aisle toward the center. The lecture hall was all long desks with three seats behind each. The width was about the same as a high school classroom, but this room was a little longer. That made it feel "long" rather than "big."

Sakuta took out his Spanish textbook and then the math book he was using at work. He opened the latter.

To prep for his evening class, he first solved the practice problem himself.

As he scribbled equations in his notes, a voice said, "Mind if I sit here?"

He looked up and blinked at the owner of the voice.

It was Miori Mitou, the girl he'd met at the party Friday. Her hair was in that same loose knot.

"I'd rather you didn't."

He'd just been accused of taking her home, after all. Evidently, he'd riled up a few of the boys. The last thing he wanted to do was subject himself to more unwarranted suspicions.

"I'm sitting here anyway," she said, tweaking her long skirt as she did.

"There's plenty of room elsewhere."

"But you're the only person here I know."

"You could have matched languages with a friend."

The language program offered more than just Spanish and Chinese—it also had German, French, Italian, etc. She'd have known she had no friends here in their first class last week.

But in lieu of an answer, she sighed dramatically.

"......"

He pretended not to hear this, going back to his math.

She sighed again, louder.

"Sorry, am I being obnoxious?"

"Not to a level worth apologizing for."

He kept solving.

"So I *am* being obnoxious, then."

"Did you get some bad news?" he asked, like he didn't care.

"Will you listen?"

"Do you want me to listen?"

"Manami and the others went to the beach over summer vacation."

"And?"

"I wasn't invited."

She pursed her lips, looking very disgruntled. She glared balefully at the mascot character on the key chain dangling from her index finger. Sakuta's eyes met the mascot's. Perhaps it was a souvenir they'd brought back for her.

"Well, if she picked Sanpo-chan, your friend has great taste."

"You know who she is?"

"I haven't lived in Fujisawa three years for nothing."

Her full name was Enoshima Sanpo-chan. A local mascot who officially and unofficially promoted the allure of Fujisawa.

"And the beach snub was probably just 'cause you don't have a phone."

This logical conclusion earned him a sidelong glare.

"What, did she come back bragging about the hunks who hit on her?"

"She didn't, so I assume nothing like that happened."

Miori looked a bit smug there. She hooked the key chain onto the fastener on her pen case.

"You act like you definitely would have been hit on if you'd been with them."

"Not acting, just thinking."

She propped her cheek up on her palm, scowling.

"So mean," he said with a laugh.

"Ugh, what even *are* friends?"

"......"

"Uh-oh, that's a 'she crazy' face."

Miori was still leaning on her arm, but her eyes had turned toward him.

"More a 'she crazy and a hassle' face."

"Now who's being mean?"

"That barely qualifies," he said, acting all modest.

This got an eye roll out of her, followed by a third sigh. This one wasn't forced; it felt like it had spilled out naturally.

"She's trying to make up for it by putting a mixer together for me."

"Isn't that nice."

"......"

Miori shot him another reproachful glare.

"If you're not into it, just tell her you don't appreciate being the bait to lure hunks to her mixer."

He figured it was a given that her name on the roster would attract next-level dudes. The vibe at last week's party had proved that.

"Who do you think I am, Azusagawa?"

"A girl so cute she'd steal all the boys without even trying, so her friends won't bring her to the beach," he said, writing the next step of the problem down in his notes.

"So harsh," she grumbled, but her tone made it clear part of her agreed with him. She was only too aware why they'd ditched her. This was likely not the first time that had happened. Nor would it be the last. And she was sick and tired of it.

"If you don't wanna, don't go to the mixer."

Then—

"A mixer? I want in!" cried a cheery new voice. And not just the voice—the whole girl leaned into the gap between them.

Sakuta and this girl went back a bit, before either of them had started college.

Her name was Uzuki Hirokawa.

"Idols aren't allowed at mixers."

"Mmph-mm-mm."

She'd probably said, "Oh, yeah, right," but this was rendered unintelligible by the bubble tea she was sipping on.

Why was Uzuki here? Simple. She was also a student at this university. Like Sakuta, she was majoring in statistical science.

Nodoka had declared early on that she was going to college, and that had turned out to be infectious. Uzuki had decided to give it a shot herself.

Nobody had told Sakuta she was even sitting the exam; at orientation, she and Nodoka had just rolled up together, and he'd been pretty surprised.

But now she misread his gaze entirely and held out her bubble tea. "Wanna sip?" she asked.

"Better not."

Indirect kisses from active idols were probably a whole thing.

"But bubble tea is da bomb!"

"Every time I drink it, I just wind up with a heap of tapioca at the end."

"But it's so good!"

"I just don't have a knack for it."

"Fair enough."

Somehow they miraculously managed to come to an understanding with that last stroke. On the surface, at least.

Uzuki inhaled some more tapioca through her straw. He could smell the sugar from here. She munched on it for a moment, looking from Sakuta to Miori and back again.

"Your new girlfriend?"

That huge pause, and all that came out after it was nonsense.

"Nope."

"She's cute."

"She's…" He trailed off, unsure how to define their relationship. No apt phrases came to mind. They'd only just met Friday and didn't really know each other yet.

"Miori Mitou," Miori said. "I'm a potential friend."

"Well, I'm Uzuki Hirokawa, and I'm *already* friends with him!"

She reached out and gave Miori an enthusiastic handshake. The up/down motion was so intense it shook Miori's head as well.

"How do you know him?" Miori asked, surviving the violent greeting.

"He's Kaede's brother!" Uzuki said, like this explained anything.

His sister had been the primary reason they got to know each other, and she still thought of him as an accessory.

"You didn't mention a sister, Azusagawa. She's friends with Hirokawa?"

"You've saved me from a lot of exposition. Yeah, Kaede's…a fan, I guess."

While Sakuta was filling Miori in, Uzuki dashed off to the front of the class.

"Everyone! Good morniiiing!"

It was almost like she was onstage and greeting her audience. The five girls clustered up front started returning the greeting.

Uzuki joined them, and they were now six, but since the other five were all dressed in matching outfits, Uzuki's thigh-hugging skinny slacks and long cardigan made her stick out like a sore thumb. Sakuta found himself remembering the ugly duckling—but this one was already a swan.

"Azusagawa," Miori said, like she was logging a complaint.

"What?"

"You know a *lot* of cute girls."

"Mitou, you're one of 'em."

"That's not how I meant it."

She glared at him like he knew better.

Then she frowned.

"Did you drop the honorific?"

"If you're a potential friend, I figured we could close the gap."

He'd finally finished solving the math problem. Now all he had to do was convey this knowledge to his students.

"*Azusagawa*'s a very long name."

"So?"

"*Azusa?*"

"Sounds like an express train."

"*Sagawa?*"

"Like the transportation company?"

"*Sakuta* feels a bit too familiar, so I guess *Azusagawa* it is."

They'd looped back around to where they began, but at this point, the Spanish professor arrived.

5

"That's all for today," the professor said in accented Japanese.

Second period started at ten thirty and wrapped up on time ninety minutes later, exactly at noon.

"¡Hasta la próxima semana!"

See you again next week. With that salutation, Professor Pedro left the podium.

"¡Hasta luego!"

This boisterous reply came from Uzuki and was accompanied by a big wave.

Pedro grinned back.

A cheery Spaniard, he meshed well with Uzuki's energy.

As Pedro left, Takumi stuck his head in the door.

"Azusagawa, lunch?" he called, moving toward Sakuta. But halfway there, his eyes turned to one side, where Miori was putting her books away.

"Chao," she said and got up to go, waving. She brushed past Takumi and vanished down the hall.

"What the hell was that, Azusagawa?" Takumi hissed, planting both hands on Sakuta's desk. "I thought you said nothing happened!"

"I've been promoted to potential friend."

"Let me in on that!"

"You'll have to ask Mitou."

"You're already that chummy with her?! I knew the man who nabbed Mai Sakurajima had game!"

His eyes had glazed over.

Up at the front of the room, other students were discussing lunch plans.

It was that group of girls again, Uzuki included.

"Cafeteria?"

"I want a *yokoichi-don!*" Uzuki said, the first to respond. This *donburi* was a school specialty. It was usually rice topped with sweet-and-spicy ground chicken, with a poached egg on top.

Just hearing the name made Sakuta want one.

"Then let's go," one of the girls said.

"Augh!" Uzuki yelped. "I've got a shoot today. I can't, sorry."

She slapped her palms together, but the girls took it in stride.

"That fashion magazine again?"

"That turned out real cute."

"I'm definitely buying a copy!"

"Same!"

"Knock 'em dead!"

"*¡Hasta mañana!*" Uzuki yelled, waving good-bye. She went running out the door.

The girls' chatter stopped dead for a moment. Then...

"You hungry?"

"School store?"

"I ate too much yesterday, so I really just wanted something small like a sandwich. Huge relief."

"Yep. Same here."

"Let's go."

A very different energy. Chuckling, they left the room.

Nobody talked about Uzuki at all.

When they were well out the door, Takumi said, "Girls scare me."

"That's just how people are."

The fact that they could pretend to be friendly when Uzuki was around seemed like a strong sign they worried about social ties less than most junior or high school kids. When the idea of a class was this rigid thing, everyone got used to drawing definitive lines and making it clear whether someone was in or out.

College made things more relaxed. Those boundaries grew fuzzier. And that worked just fine.

"You scare me sometimes, too," Takumi said.

"The cafeteria's filling up fast."

The cafeteria was down the row of trees from the clock tower. You turned left at the end, and it was up ahead, on the first floor of a building with a large hall and a number of different shops.

It was peak lunch rush, and all four hundred seats were full. Finding anywhere to sit was a struggle.

Sakuta managed to snag a table as three other boys left, and Takumi joined him, bringing an extra tray for Sakuta.

They were both eating *yokoichi-don*.

The regular size was a low three hundred yen. The cafeteria menu was generally quite affordable, with soba and udon dishes going for less than two hundred yen. The school lunchroom was a vital ally to any starving student.

Every now and then you'd see parents with kids or groups of old ladies coming through who didn't really seem like they belonged, but the cafeteria was open to the public, and they were welcome, too. These days, many universities were trying things like this out, hoping to earn some goodwill in the neighborhood. That motivated lots of schools to remodel their cafeterias to look like fancy cafés. They'd get featured on TV sometimes.

It took maybe five minutes for them to empty their bowls. They washed it all down with free tea from the bar.

"Azusagawa, you gotta introduce me to a girl." This was Takumi's default conversation opener.

"Didn't you get numbers at the party?"

"Nobody's answering."

"Rough."

"I'll settle for Toyohama."

"If she even hears you say her name and *settle* in the same sentence, she'll snap. It's not hard to make her snap."

He took another sip of tea. Then something glittering at the entrance caught his eye. Speak of the devil.

She wasn't the only person on campus with blond locks, but she was definitely taking care of them better than anyone else. At school, she always bunched them low and let them hang in front of her shoulders.

Nodoka looked around the cafeteria, searching for someone.

As soon as her eyes met Sakuta's, she headed his way. Apparently, she'd been looking for him.

"There you are!" she said, like it was his fault she couldn't find him right away.

"Whatcha need?"

Nodoka glanced over at Takumi.

"Gotta borrow Sakuta for a bit," she said.

"Go right ahead. Help yourself!"

So easily relinquished.

Without any confirmation from Sakuta himself, Nodoka did an about-face and stalked off to the exit. She'd be livid if he didn't follow, so he dropped his dishes in the deposit area and hurried after her.

Outside, Sakuta and Nodoka strolled absentmindedly over to a bench by the research building and sat down on it. Nearby, the dance club was using the building windows as a mirror, rehearsing their routines.

They watched that for a while, but Nodoka didn't say anything.

"So?" Sakuta asked.

"…You saw Uzuki today?"

"I did. She was in Spanish with me."

Nodoka knew that, which was why she'd been looking for him.

"She say anything?"

"Like what?"

"……"

"You hauled me all the way out here. Don't be coy."

"How was she acting?"

His flippant jab didn't lighten her mood. She didn't take her eyes off the dancers.

"She seemed like she always does."

Sakuta hadn't picked up on anything wrong.

Her barging into his conversation with Miori, offering a sip of bubble tea, then dashing off to the group of girls, enthusiastically using all the new Spanish she'd learned…and the way the girls had dropped her the second she left the room. All of that was typical Uzuki.

"She didn't mention me?"

"Nope."

"Or Sweet Bullet?"

"Not a word."

"Oh..."

He was still lost.

"What's this about?" he asked.

She finally turned to look at him. The look in her eyes was half-angry, half-lost.

"Yesterday, we kinda..."

"Kinda what?"

"Had a fight."

"A fight?"

There were two reasons why that didn't seem real to him. First, he simply couldn't picture Nodoka and Uzuki going at it.

Second, the way Uzuki had acted today—she'd been totally normal. The total opposite of Nodoka's gloomy disposition, which made him feel like there must be some mistake.

"What about?" he asked.

"...You know two of our members already graduated?"

"Yeah."

Nodoka and Uzuki were both members of an idol group called Sweet Bullet.

At the start of the school year, two of the seven members had left the group ("graduated"), leaving five behind.

"Since that happened, we've been having talks among ourselves and with the agency...about our future."

"One of those 'break up or keep going' deals?"

"......"

She neither confirmed nor denied. Her silence suggested she wasn't happy with where things stood, which was all the answer he needed.

"Our goal was to play the Budokan in three years."

She used the past tense because that date had come and gone. That had probably forced them to take stock.

"But your fans and gigs are still on the upswing, right?"

They'd played a big music festival that summer and done a head-lining tour of the major cities. Kaede had brought her friend Kotomi

Kano to see them in T⟨...⟩ They'd filled two thousand seats, and
it had apparently been pre⟨...⟩ild. Kaede had been super pumped
up about it when she got bac⟨...⟩
Just...amazing!" d kept going, "It was so much fun!

And the individual members we⟨...⟩etting work. Uzuki was making
a name for herself on game shows ⟨...⟩ the like, and she was doing
more guest spots on about-town show⟨...⟩ pieces. Her unpredictable
behavior won her smiles wherever she wen⟨...⟩

Nodoka was often paired with her, keeping⟨...⟩er in line, and the contrast between Nodoka's wild appearance and ea⟨...⟩est nature was quite popular.

The other members were doing modeling work, ⟨t⟩aking acting jobs, or throwing themselves into spots on athletic variety shows—everyone was getting opportunities.

But they were still the kinda group that only the fans recognized.

"Yeah, so we had a talk about what to do as Sweet Bullet. Uzuki in particular has a lot of offers...and it's getting harder to align her schedule with the rest of us. The agency has thoughts on that, too."

"Thoughts?"

"...Like having her go solo," Nodoka muttered.

She stifled all her emotions, trying her best to sound and act normal.

"Yesterday, we had a concert with other agency groups. And I heard the chief director on the phone with someone."

He was starting to see how they'd wound up fighting.

"The agency aside, Hirokawa knew about this?"

"She probably doesn't."

He'd figured. If she had, that would be a whole different problem.

"What do *you* want?"

"I...I still wanna play the Budokan. As Sweet Bullet."

But Nodoka's eyes had turned back to the dance club.

"But at the same time, I want everyone's hard work to pay off. Uzuki's worked harder than anyone else, and...she really has something, you know? She brings a smile to everyone's face."

"Mm-hmm. And you tried to tell h̶ ̶ ̶ ̶at in a roundabout way, but she didn't get it at all, and you foun̶ ̶urself losing your temper and lashing out at her?"

Nodoka might have a flashy lo̶ but deep down she was a very serious person. Her concern for U̶ki had likely gone unnoticed and led to her saying things she regr̶ed.

"…Basically, yeah."

That explained why N̶doka had called it a fight. But the heightened emotions had a̶ been on her side. Uzuki had been wholly unconcerned today̶ because she didn't know about the solo offer and hadn't known w̶at to make of their difference of opinion.

"Everyone else felt like I did, so…it wound up feeling like we'd all turned on her."

And she felt guilty about that, couldn't quite face Uzuki herself, and was using Sakuta as a cushion.

"Is that all?"

"Huh?"

Nodoka scowled at him, clearly wanting more.

"This is a real problem!"

"A first world problem."

"……"

"You're basically griping because you've got more work and things can't be how they've always been. If you told Mai that, she'd slap you."

"Ugh, yeah…"

Sakuta had a sinking feeling it would somehow end with him getting slapped instead. He definitely didn't want her catching word of this.

"……"

Nodoka had definitely heard him but wasn't quite swallowing it.

"If you're super hung up on Hirokawa, go talk to her again. Don't go sneaking around picking the brains of unrelated dudes."

"You be quiet! I know that much."

He'd managed to get under her skin, and she jumped to her feet.

"Only a dumbass would talk to *you*," she said. "Thanks!"

Was she mad at him or grateful? Her emotions were swirling every which way as she stomped off.

One of the dancing girls shot him a look like, "What did you do?" When Sakuta caught her looking, she hastily averted her eyes.

"I don't need to be any more notorious than I already am…"

He felt like Nodoka had it together a little better now that she was in college, but…not when she was with him.

"Which is fine."

He got up and stretched.

The rain that morning had left the air feeling clean.

The story he'd just heard was like the weather. Emotions were like the sun, the clouds, and the rain. He could let Nodoka and Uzuki be, and it would all work out. Today had just been some bad weather.

Those two weren't just any old run-of-the-mill friends. They were part of the same group, working toward the same goal. They'd been through thick and thin together and forged bonds of trust.

They might not be friends, but they could lean on each other.

They might not be besties, but they could support each other.

He knew they'd built something stronger.

Changes around them would not be enough to shatter that now.

At the time, Sakuta genuinely believed that.

Believed this was a trivial concern.

That it would blow over.

But things have a way of turning out differently.

And the next day, they did.

The campus might not have looked different, but the change itself was all too clear.

Chapter
2
catching the wavelength

1

The next day was October 4, and Sakuta greeted it like any other morning.

First, he woke up to Nasuno pawing his face. She meowed once, demanding breakfast, and that forced him up and into the living room. He poured some dry food into her bowl, then got breakfast for two on the table. At the same time, he made himself a lunch. Best to save money where you could.

He ate breakfast alone, then went to the door with his sister's name on it, calling out, "Kaede, it's morning."

She didn't answer, and he didn't open the door.

The whole teenager thing seemed to have caught up with Kaede at last, and if he opened the door unbidden, he'd have his ear chewed off.

So he left her to it.

After a long minute, she emerged, mumbling, "Mornin', Sakuta."

Her eyes were definitely not open.

"Make sure you wash the plate after."

"*Yawn*... Okay, see you later."

She saw him out the door with another yawn.

It was mostly sunny.

There were clouds like strings of cotton candy, but plenty of blue beyond. The air itself was dry, and it felt like fall was finally here. Beneath that beautiful backdrop, he made his way to Fujisawa Station. There, he took the JR Tokaido Line to Yokohama Station and changed to the Keikyu Line for another twenty-minute ride. He got off at Kanazawa-hakkei Station, where his university's gates awaited. It was a solid hour commute from home.

Outside the station gates, a crowd of students were streaming toward the campus.

Some spotted friends along the way and called out to them, while others were talking or texting on their phones. A few were walking quietly, listening to their headphones. Sakuta was one of several stifling a yawn, fighting off the urge to sleep.

This was what he saw every morning.

Inside the main gates, there were even more students, and the campus buzzed with energy. It always did.

His college looked just like it had yesterday.

As did the students.

Some people would grow bored with the student routine. He often heard people grumble about how they thought college life was supposed to be a lot more fun.

But Sakuta wasn't one to complain about a little tedium.

Nothing happening meant things were good.

All was as it should be.

His mind on these things, Sakuta passed through the familiar sights into the building where his second-period class was held.

Up the stairs, he turned into room 201. Here, Sakuta had to take a required class that covered linear algebra.

Maybe a third of the seats were full. Everyone here was in his major. Mostly first-years. There were four or five second-years who'd failed the class last year—a fact that had come out during the orientation lecture last week. The professor had warned them not to fail it a second time.

He saw a familiar back in the center of the room.

Takumi.

Sakuta headed his way. Takumi spotted him and raised a hand.

"'Sup," he said, and shifted one seat down the row. "Warmed that seat for ya," he said.

It was far too early to savor the warmth of another man's ass, so Sakuta said, "Cool," and sat down one row farther in.

"You got something against me?" Takumi asked.

"I just like my seats ice-cold."

"Like your beers!"

While they bantered about nothing, Sakuta opened the linear algebra textbook and took out his notes. The textbook they were using bore the name of the professor teaching it. This was not the only class that worked like that; quite a few college professors wrote their own textbooks. And they earned royalties for the purchases, which seemed like one way to keep the world going round.

Sakuta absentmindedly glanced at the clock. It was 10:25. Five minutes till class started.

Shrill laughter from the front of the room drew his eye. It was that group of girls, once again all dressed alike. They were doing something on their phones—taking short videos and showing them to each other. Uzuki was with them.

Two rows back, a boy had his nose in a book. He kept grinning, so it probably wasn't anything deep.

The student next to him had his head down, sound asleep. Before class could even begin. Bold.

Most everyone else was playing with their phones or chatting with a friend.

It was all typical pre-class stuff. Nothing weird about it. But something about this scene was bugging Sakuta.

Something about one girl had struck him as odd. Still did.

He focused on one of the six girls in the group up front. She was wearing the same kind of skirt they were. The same kind of blouse. It was Uzuki.

She was riffing off her friends' jokes and feeding them setups, laughing with the same timing they had.

That itself was typical behavior for any group of girls. Something you saw all the time around campus. Nothing weird about it. That's why he couldn't quite figure out why it was bugging him. He didn't know what seemed so off here.

He sat watching Uzuki, feeling like he was playing a super tough game of spot the difference. Eventually, she felt him staring, and her eyes met his.

Any other day, she'd have waved enthusiastically and called out to him, drawing so much attention it sort of made him wince.

But today, she was acting different. She looked at Sakuta, and her mouth opened slightly like she'd just remembered something. Then she said, "Gimme a minute," and moved away from her friends.

She came right over to Sakuta and glanced around quickly to see if anyone was watching. Then she leaned in and whispered, "You hear from Nodoka?"

Softly enough that only he could hear.

"Should I have?" he asked, unsure what she meant.

"Shoulda coulda woulda."

That rhymed, but it didn't clear much up.

"I'm lost," Sakuta said.

Uzuki made a face at him, but he genuinely didn't know what she was after here.

"Something go down between you two?"

Nodoka *had* told him about their "fight," and he couldn't imagine anything else this could be.

But in his mind, that problem was already solved. He and Nodoka had talked about it, and she said she was gonna work it out with Uzuki—so there was nothing left for *him* to do.

"I was busy with my shoot all day yesterday, so I haven't seen her yet."

"Or heard from her?"

"Not yesterday."

Curious phrasing. If she specified yesterday, that made it sound like she had today. And Sakuta's suspicion proved warranted.

"I just got a text from her asking if I was on campus today," Uzuki added.

"And?"

"A question like that makes it sound like she needs to *talk*."

"Not sure that's universally true."

He didn't think Uzuki would have taken it that way a day before. She'd have shot back, "What's up, Nodoka?!" before any conjecture. If she'd been in a position to call, she probably would have rung her on the spot. Not probably—definitely.

And that made him think something was up with her again.

"Hirokawa, are you sure nothing happened with you yesterday?" he asked.

"What would?"

"Woulda coulda shoulda."

"You're copying me!"

She laughed, like she was trying to lighten the mood. That also seemed off to him. Uzuki, faking a smile? He'd never seen her do that. At least, not until today.

And if asked if something happened, the Uzuki Hirokawa he knew would have blown right through whatever he meant by the question, blurting, "I fell over during the shoot and hit my butt!" or whatever else popped into her head.

Why did this feel so wrong?

He was still trying to work it out when she laughed again and said, "I'm in good form today."

She was looking away, at the girls up front.

"Like I'm on their wavelength."

He looked her over again, and she was definitely dressed the way they were.

"Looks like," he said.

Maybe there were just days like that.

But even Uzuki seemed to think she was different. Feeling like she was in sync with the girls, performing better than usual socially.

While he mulled that over, the professor came in, softly saying, "Take your seats."

The students faced front, and Uzuki dashed back up to her friends.

"Yo, Fukuyama," Sakuta said over his shoulder, eyes on Uzuki's back.

"Mm?"

"What'd you make of her today?"

"She was cute."

"Anything else?"

"She was *cute*."

That sure sounded like Takumi.

"A valuable take, thanks."

"You're welcome."

Sakuta glanced around and confirmed that no one else seemed concerned about her. Only he felt anything was amiss.

Maybe it was all in his head.

It could just be coincidence that they'd all dressed alike and were laughing at the same things. Maybe it was pure chance she'd just happened to worry about Nodoka's text.

She was in good form.

And Sakuta was probably overthinking it.

Hoping that was the case, he opened his linear algebra book.

2

But however trivial, once something started itching at him, he couldn't stop scratching it. He spent the whole class with his eyes on Uzuki, watching for anything else out of place.

Until yesterday, Uzuki would have listened with rapt attention. If she didn't get something, she'd have thrown a hand up even if that meant interrupting class. Even if the friends around her were whispering or texting one another, once she found her focus, she stayed that way. That was how Uzuki did things.

But today, she was fidgeting constantly, joking with the friend next to her. Sometimes, she'd crook her head at what the teacher said, but she didn't call out, "I don't get it!"

When class ended, she didn't wave the teacher out or yell, "See you next week!"

Like everyone else here, she just put her books away and joined the girls around her, talking about where to get lunch. Her voice didn't echo above the crowd. Someone suggested the cafeteria, and she just said, "Mm, let's do that," using an indoor voice.

And this all just made Sakuta certain something was wrong. But once again, only he seemed to have noticed.

The girls around her were talking like she was always this way. "Let's swing through Yokohama on the way home," one suggested, and it sounded so natural that it didn't feel like they were putting on an act.

From another perspective, this was a typical college-girl conversation, nothing extraordinary about it. The way Uzuki usually tried to join in while being constantly a bit more wound up than anyone else—that was far less natural.

His thoughts were interrupted by a voice behind him. Takumi, asking, "Azusagawa, lunch?"

Sakuta turned to look and found Takumi leaning way over the seat.

"I brought lunch today," he said.

"Enough for me?"

"It'd be creepy if I had."

"True. I'd die."

Takumi sat back up.

"Gonna hit the shop, then," he said, and then he was out the back door. He said it like he'd be right back, so Sakuta figured he should wait.

But a blond girl came in the door he'd vacated.

Nodoka.

She looked at Sakuta for one second but quickly turned to Uzuki— who was about to head out the front door.

"Uzuki," she called.

Uzuki flinched. Then she said, "Sorry, you go on ahead," to her friends and sent them into the hall.

Most of the other students had gone to lunch, too. Sakuta had put his lunch box on his desk, but that left him alone with two idols.

"......"

"......"

One at the front of the room, one at the back. That distance and tension separated them.

"Guess I'll...go buy a drink," Sakuta said, attempting to take the hint. But Nodoka cut him off.

"I haven't opened this yet," she said.

She moved forward to his row and dropped a soda bottle next to him. Peach flavor—Mai had done a commercial for it not long ago.

If she wanted him here, he was happy to sit, but...

"Uh, Nodoka, is this about the thing?" Uzuki asked, going first.

"The thing?" Nodoka repeated, frowning.

"Sunday, 'course."

Uzuki was talking like this was *obvious*.

"......?"

And that's why Nodoka looked baffled. She hadn't expected Uzuki to bring it up first. She'd just assumed her irritation, concern, anxiety, and worries had been totally lost on her. And she'd said as much the day before.

"I'm super sorry!" Uzuki said, slapping both hands together. Nodoka got even more confused. "I had no idea what you were all going through! Of course you're mad."

"...Uzuki?"

"We get so many jobs that drag us off in different directions, we're spending a lot less time together. I don't want that, either, so let's make sure we talk about that as a group."

"Uh, great, but, um. I'm sorry, too. I didn't mean to say all that."

"Don't worry about it. You speaking up clued me in."

"Okay…"

"I mean, solo work matters, too? These jobs help more people find out about Sweet Bullet."

"I totally agree."

"But if that pulls us apart, it's not worth it."

"Mm…"

"So let's meet up with Yae, Ranko, and Hotaru. Everyone'll be at the dance lesson today, right?"

"That's what I hear…"

Who was she talking to here?

There was a good chance Nodoka was wondering that.

Uzuki was speaking very logically, and Nodoka looked stunned the whole time.

"Nodoka? Am I saying something weird?"

Nodoka wasn't reacting much, and Uzuki picked up on that. That itself was the root of why this felt so strange. She was perfectly tailoring what she said to the person she was talking to.

"No, that's basically everything I meant to say," Nodoka managed.

"Great."

"Mm."

Nodoka had been totally out of it this whole time.

"Nodoka?" Uzuki frowned, not missing that, either.

"Nothing… Um, Yae's got a shoot, so she'll be a little late, but we can talk then. I'll let the others know."

"Cool! Do that. I'm gonna go eat lunch with my friends."

Uzuki waved, grabbed her bag, and ran off. She was soon out of sight.

"……"

"……"

They were left feeling bamboozled, unsure how they were supposed to feel. Confused? Surprised? Did that really just happen? It was hard to be sure. It didn't sit right. It left them with serious *doubts*.

Unable to sort it out, Nodoka just stood there staring at the door. It was like she never planned to move again.

"That went well," Sakuta said.

"……"

Nodoka's eyes swiveled toward him, questions plastered on her face.

"I said, that went well."

"What did?"

"You made up."

"…Right. Yes, we did."

Nodoka nodded, but her frown didn't go away. It still wasn't adding up.

"The hell *was* that?!"

The words burst out of her. If he'd said anything himself, it probably would have sounded like that. If Sakuta had been in her position, that's exactly what he'd be doing.

"Sakuta, what did you say to her?" Nodoka's tone sounded accusatory.

"Not a thing."

"Really?"

"I swear."

"Then how is she like this about stuff she totally didn't get on Sunday?"

"If you don't know, how should I?"

"Huh?"

"You know her better than I do."

They'd met long before he knew either of them and had spent a *lot* of time together.

"Obviously!" Nodoka snapped, but she was agreeing with him.

That didn't make it any less weird, though. She thought for a minute.

"Are we sure that was Uzuki?" she asked, dead serious.

"Who else would it be?"

"She was, like, watching my reactions while she talked."

The way she put it made it sound like that was *not* like Uzuki at all.

"She was."

"But that means…"

The words got stuck in her throat, and she broke off. Hesitant to say it out loud.

"Uzuki's reading the room!"

That was what she eventually settled on.

"Yep."

That's all there was to it.

Only one thing had changed.

Nodoka had hit the nail on the head.

She'd read the room.

Uzuki.

That was what had felt so wrong.

"Are we sure this isn't like what happened to me and Mai?" Nodoka demanded.

"Like a body swap?"

"Mm."

"She knew too much about Sweet Bullet's business."

What they'd just talked about was all insider stuff.

"True…"

"Even if this is some kinda Adolescence Syndrome, is it a bad thing?"

"Well…"

From her tone, she'd been about to say, "Well, yeah!" But before she did, her brain caught up.

She'd patched things over with Uzuki.

Because Uzuki had worked out why Nodoka had been so upset.

That wasn't a problem for anyone.

It was actually a net benefit for all.

That had certainly rattled Nodoka.

But Uzuki herself had said she was in good form now that she was on the same wavelength as everyone. She'd been happy about it.

But the change had been dramatic enough to shake both Nodoka and Sakuta to their cores.

"Then…I guess we can let it be?"

Nodoka didn't sound at all sure of herself.

"She might be her old self again tomorrow," he suggested. And that was how they punted the problem down the road.

3

Ultimately, Sakuta's forlorn hopes were dashed, and Uzuki was still tuned to that wavelength the next day.

He woke at six, got ready, and headed in to a first-period class. Uzuki was smoothly blending in with the girls from their major.

They were all dressed alike, chattering about the same topics, laughing in sync.

And that still felt wrong to him.

Late last night, after the dance lesson, Nodoka had called him and said they'd all had a good talk.

Their time together as Sweet Bullet mattered.

And so did the work they did on their own.

Giving their all on every job currently on their collective plates was the only real way to spread word about their group.

And by talking things out, they were more tight-knit than ever. Nodoka sounded upbeat and cheerful the whole time. They'd always had trouble getting on the same page with Uzuki; her priorities just never quite aligned with the others. But now Uzuki *got it*.

Whatever this mess was, it had had only upsides.

Seeing Uzuki cheerily laughing with her friends was kind of a relief. A few days back, she'd been clearly out of place, and that had felt risky, or at least uncomfortable. None of that remained. They were even-keeled and steady.

Unfortunately, seeing Uzuki just...fit in was itself a source of discomfort.

No one but Sakuta seemed bothered by this change. Most likely, they weren't interested enough to notice. Everyone had their comfort zone staked out and didn't care what happened around them as long as that remained undisturbed. Maybe if he acted like he didn't care, one day he'd actually stop caring.

If it were anyone but Uzuki, Sakuta himself probably wouldn't have noticed or cared.

"Hey, Fukuyama," he said. Takumi was sitting next to him.

"Mm?"

He'd made a very sleepy noise. Takumi's eyes were only half-open.

"What do you make of Hirokawa today?"

"She's cute."

"Anything else?"

"She's *cute*."

"I thought so."

"Man, Azusagawa…" He must have woken up a bit, because his eyes were focused now.

"Mm?" This time it was Sakuta who sounded sleepy.

"Was there a correct answer to that question?"

It had been the second day in a row, so he was right to wonder.

"Cute is fine," Sakuta said, stifling a yawn.

"You sure about that?"

It wasn't like Sakuta had an answer in mind.

When he said nothing else, Takumi's frown deepened.

After surviving first- *and* second-period classes, Sakuta headed to the cafeteria. He'd woken up at six and made a lunch, but Mai was on campus today, and they'd agreed to eat together.

The cafeteria was already 80 percent full.

He looked around the crowd and found Mai. She'd nabbed a window seat and was waving him over.

Sakuta threaded his way through the tray-bearing students to her table—and realized someone else was sitting across from Mai.

She had her back to Sakuta, but he recognized her anyway. For the simple reason that this was Miori Mitou, his newly anointed potential friend.

As he neared the table, she called out, "Oh, Azusagawa! What's up?"

Sakuta glanced at each of them, then sat down next to Mai.

"We were in second-period English together," Mai said before he could ask.

"When Mai sat down next to me, my heart nearly leaped out of my chest."

Miori put her hands over her heart, like it was trying to escape again.

"You're so dramatic, Miori," Mai scoffed.

"No, no, you shouldn't underestimate the effect you have on people, Mai. Right, Azusagawa?"

The rejoinder felt natural, and so did her toss to him. Mai's eyes turned toward him, too.

Sakuta glanced at each again, then voiced his honest opinion. "You sure made friends fast."

They'd both ordered the cafeteria's exclusive *donburi* and already polished it off. Not a kernel of rice left. And given the table location, their second-period class must have wrapped up early. They'd likely talked quite a bit before he got here.

"Are you jealous?" Miori asked.

"Mai's not great at making friends, so consider me surprised."

He took his lunch out of his backpack and put it on the table.

"That is not true," Mai said, feigning anger.

She used this as an excuse to swipe a piece of rolled egg from his lunch.

"They paired us up for conversation practice, so we were talking the whole time," she said, then popped the egg in her mouth. "Mm, that's good."

Sakuta had taken English last semester. They allowed no Japanese in class, so your partner was everything. That had been a big part of why Sakuta and Takumi were still talking.

"Then I heard she didn't own a phone and realized this was the girl you'd mentioned."

"I bet he told you I was a glutton who wolfed down three chicken nuggets."

"I swear I didn't."

"Well, it helped me get closer to Mai, so you're forgiven."

Miori wasn't paying him any heed.

But either way, that meant Mai and Miori were weirdly chummy. Mai was definitely not someone who jumped straight to a first-name basis often. She'd been quite distant with Sakuta for quite a while.

"When Miori introduced herself, she said to use her first name. I was a little reluctant, but…when you're speaking English, that's how it's done."

"Why'd you insist?" Sakuta asked.

"I just wanted to hear my name on Mai's lips," Miori replied, not missing a beat.

"I hear that," Sakuta said, digging into his lunch.

Mai got up without a word and came back with tea. She set it down next to his lunch.

"Thanks, Mai."

Her lips curled slightly. A gentle smile.

"……"

Miori was blinking at them.

"What now, Miori?"

"…You really *are* a couple."

She blinked again, like she couldn't believe her eyes.

"Everyone agrees she's too good for me."

Few people were rude enough to say so, but their glares spoke volumes. This wasn't out of the ordinary. He didn't think anyone had genuinely said they made a cute couple. Certainly not any friends or acquaintances he'd made at college.

"No, I don't mean that. Like…the way you act with each other is natural. You're clearly a good match."

She sounded a bit formal and a little embarrassed. Like saying that aloud was awkward for her. Complimenting people could be weirdly stressful like that.

"Thanks, Miori," Mai said, smiling at her.

Miori toppled over in her seat like she'd been shot through the heart.

"Hang in there," Sakuta said.

"I can't! I'm in love!"

"Like I said, Mai's mine, and you can't have her."

"Can I borrow her sometimes?"

"I belong to *nobody*," Mai said.

Miori straightened up, looking tense.

"Don't sweat it, Miori. Mai doesn't get mad that easily."

"Yes, Sakuta is never not a snot."

Mai's chopsticks shot toward his lunch again, swiping a frozen crab cream croquette. Kaede was addicted to the things, and there was always a bunch in the freezer at home.

"Argh, Mai! At least leave me half!"

But his pleas went unheeded, and Mai ate the whole thing.

"...This is weird—like, am I allowed to be here?"

Miori was looking back and forth between them, as if feeling insecure.

"Probably best you leave."

"Absolutely stay."

Sakuta and Mai spoke on top of each other.

"I'm gonna go get a refill," Miori said, splitting the difference. She grabbed Mai's empty cup, too, not missing a beat.

"She's a bit like you," Mai said as she watched her walk away.

"Don't tell Mitou. She'd probably hate it."

"But you don't. I mean, she's cute."

Miori came back with more tea.

"Whatcha talking about?" she asked, plopping the plastic cups down on the table.

"How you're cute."

"Mai, is that true?"

Miori clearly didn't believe him. Sakuta had not earned her trust.

"Yes."

"Well, thank you, then."

Mai, she believed. Miori settled back down and took a sip of tea to cover her blush.

There was a brief lull in conversation, and Sakuta took the opportunity to finish off the rolled eggs. He put his chopsticks back in their case and closed the lid on his lunch box, then wrapped it up in the cloth.

He took a sip of the tea Mai had brought him.

His eyes wandered around the cafeteria and stopped on a table two spots down. Like theirs, it was a four-seater. Four girls were sitting there, in similar outfits and with similar makeup. Based on the dishes, they'd all ordered the same thing.

"High school was easier," Miori said out of nowhere.

"Mm?"

He glanced her way, confused, and she was looking at the same table.

"Everyone was in uniform."

"Oh."

She'd clearly followed his gaze and guessed what it meant. Figuring that made it okay, he looked again. Upon closer examination, the table behind them held a pair of girls who were also dressed alike.

He glanced around the cafeteria and saw quite a few tables like this. If this were poker, there were any number of flushes, full houses, three or four of a kind, two pairs, or one pair—he couldn't be bothered to count them all.

"Do they, like, talk it over and decide these things?"

"As if anyone would do something that annoying."

"I didn't think so."

Even Sakuta couldn't picture anyone texting people every morning to decide the collective look of the day.

But they sure lined up a lot for pure coincidence. It was kinda uncanny, really.

"I struggle with it every morning. Don't want anyone thinking I'm drab, but don't want anyone laughing because I'm trying too hard."

Miori was wearing a dress with a relaxed denim shirt over it. The dress alone would have been trying too hard, so she'd added the shirt to tone it down.

He glanced around and found other girls dressed like her.

"You do it, too, Azusagawa."

She glanced at a pair of dudes over his shoulder. Navy ankle pants, long-sleeved T-shirts. Exactly like what he had on. Even their backpacks were black.

He got her point without her spelling it out.

"I consulted my wallet, went to a store, and bought what the mannequin had on. This is the result."

"I'm also wearing a mannequin look," Miori laughed, plucking her clothes. "And what I wore yesterday came up when I googled 'fall college outfits.' If you shop in the same places and look at the same sites, you end up dressing the same."

"I guess."

"And if you're like everyone else, nobody'll laugh. No reason to dress different here. Back in high school, everyone was hiking their skirts up, loosening their neckties, swapping out their socks, desperate to find some way to stand out."

Miori winced at the memories.

But that's just how people are. The moment they're given freedom to choose, they feel like they're being put to the test and shrink back. As long as they're doing what someone else decided, they could shift the blame. But if it's *their* choice, there'd be no excuses, no escape routes.

"You don't have a phone, but you still google things."

"I've got a computer at home."

That wasn't really anything to be smug about, but she put her hands on her hips and puffed out her chest. Apparently, she wasn't diametrically opposed to the Internet itself.

"Where do you buy your clothes, Mai?" Miori asked.

Mai had been listening in silence. "Me?"

"You always look cute. I'd love to know."

"Mai *is* always cute."

Today Mai was wearing a collared blouse with a sweater vest over it. And a long skirt below that. Her hair was done up in two loose braids, which were draped over her shoulders. And with her fake glasses, she had that literature-club vibe going.

One false move, and the whole thing would look dowdy, but Mai pulled it off with mature elegance.

"I often buy outfits from fashion shoots direct from the stylist. This outfit is one of those."

"Can't copy that!" Miori hung her head. "But even if I could, I'm not you, so it probably wouldn't work."

Now she was sulking.

"You'd be surprised."

"What do you know, Azusagawa? Have you tried?"

"Yes."

"Creepy..."

"My sister, I mean. She gets a lot of Mai's hand-me-downs."

Kaede was surprisingly tall, so she could wear a lot of what Mai did. Sometimes that made her look like she was being dressed up for something, but most of them worked fine.

"Lucky sister. If I were your sister... Ew, I don't want that, but still...jealous."

"Talk about mixed messages."

"What *were* we talking about anyway?" Miori asked, letting his words go in one ear and out the other.

"You suddenly started waxing nostalgic about high school uniforms."

"Because you were looking at the other table," Mai said, glancing at the girls who had prompted this whole thing.

"Oh, right. Azusagawa, what caught your attention?"

"Meaning?"

"Meaning what I said."

"No real reason."

He shifted his gaze away evasively, and Miori seemed to buy it for now. Or at least, she didn't try to dig further.

At this point, the bell rang, warning that break was almost over. The students loitering in the cafeteria started moving out.

"I've gotta return a book to the library," Miori said, getting up first.

"I'll clear your dishes," Sakuta said as he reached for her tray.

"Oh, thanks."

"See you in class next week," Mai said.

Miori waved and left the room.

He watched her go, then dropped off her tray.

Sakuta and Mai left together and walked over to the main building.

"You have afternoon classes, Sakuta?"

"I'm happy to blow them off and go on a date with you."

He glanced up through the trees; the skies were blue.

Perfect date weather.

A few days before, it had still felt hot, but now it was properly cool for fall.

"If you're here till fourth period, we could go home together."

"Third period's my last one, but I've gotta prep for cram school, so I can wait for you."

"Oh? But you've got work, then."

"Yeah, shame. I was hoping I'd get to feast on you alongside your dinner tonight."

"If you talk like that, I'm not coming to cook."

"Aww."

"If you see Futaba at work, maybe talk to her about the thing?"

"Mm?"

"That whole tangent was about Hirokawa, right?"

He'd figured Mai knew. And that was why she hadn't asked. Nodoka must have told her something.

"I'll run it by her, yeah. She'll roll her eyes so hard."

4

"So you're *still* in the throes of adolescence," Rio said.

He'd filled her in on Uzuki, and that was her first reaction.

They'd each finished up their lessons for the day.

They were in a family restaurant, which was still 80 percent full even at ten PM.

Kaede was working today, and she'd taken their orders. But it was his old kohai Tomoe Koga who brought their food. Neither one of them was on the floor now. High school students could only work till ten. They were both in the staff room, getting ready to head home.

"I've retained my childish innocence."

"And you're weirdly sensitive for a rascal."

"Haven't heard that word in a while."

Rio ignored this. "It sounds like just what you think it is," she said.

"Meaning?"

"An idol who couldn't read the room learned how."

"Is that even possible?"

Uzuki's ditziness had been just that ingrained. Not something she could just fix overnight.

"You're hell-bent on tying this to Adolescence Syndrome, huh?"

"I mean, I'm hoping it isn't."

He meant this.

He'd gone a year and a half without encountering any and would happily stay that way.

But it was also true that Uzuki's thing made a lot more sense if it *was* Adolescence Syndrome. That's how uncanny her transformation was.

"Even if it *was* Adolescence Syndrome, she wasn't worried about her ditziness, right?"

"Right."

She likely had been at one point. Unable to converse with her peers or make friends, she'd found herself isolated. Uzuki herself had said she spent junior and senior high like that.

But before she met Sakuta, she'd dropped out of conventional schooling, switched to remote learning, and moved past it.

She'd obtained happiness on her own terms.

Her mom had helped her find it in her.

That side of Uzuki had been a goalpost for Kaede when she was struggling with not being like other people. She'd given Kaede courage. And that had made his sister into a lifelong fan.

"So I don't see a reason why she'd get Adolescence Syndrome."

"Exactly."

Talking to Rio had brought him to the same conclusion. There was no problem. And that felt like a problem. But if there wasn't a problem, then how could there be a problem? Was this a Zen koan?

"You don't look satisfied."

"Well, no. If it was *just* reading the room, then fine. But doesn't it creep you out a bit that her clothing suddenly started matching everyone else's?"

Even now, there was a group of three college girls at a nearby table, all sporting a similar look. Knee-length skirts, fancy blouses, hair gently curled around their shoulders. Makeup that made their cheeks look slightly flushed like they'd just stepped out of the bath. They were happily chitchatting, doing a postmortem on a mixer—or rather, dissing all the disappointing men they'd met there.

"I think this new cute girl you're friends with hit the nail on the head there."

Rio sounded a bit curt. She took a sip of her coffee. There was a hint of color on her lips. She kept it subtle, but Rio had started wearing makeup in college, too.

"She's still just a potential friend."

"But you don't deny the cute part."

"What nail on what head?"

Better to move the conversation along before she needled him any further.

"If you're looking at the same sources, even if you don't directly discuss it, that shared info will put you all in the same ballpark. A natural outcome of basic social skills."

Rio acted like this didn't affect her, but this perception was exactly what was bugging Sakuta.

"But isn't that a *lot* like quantum entanglement?"

In that state, particles could instantly share information and behavior without the advent of a connective medium. Rio had told him about this.

"If you bend the results to your desired interpretation, maybe. That's as far as I'm willing to go."

She looked up from her coffee and surreptitiously glanced at the table in back.

"Let's say there's a community in a state of quantum entanglement."

Rio's eyes were on the girls who'd come from a mixer.

"Okay."

"They meet up with a friend who *isn't* entangled."

This was nicely timed—a fourth girl arrived late, joining her friends. They'd come up empty at the mixer and called in other friends. But this friend alone was wearing a military-surplus jacket, and she stuck out like a sore thumb.

"So I see."

"And if this late arrival happens to get dragged into the entanglement phenomenon, she'll end up sharing information and syncing with the community. So I *do* get where you're coming from, Azusagawa."

The late arrival took off her jacket the moment she sat down. Beneath it, she was wearing exactly what the other three were.

It was like she'd synchronized with them, becoming one with their group.

Simply a result of everyone getting on the same wavelength.

That made it sound like no big deal, but reading the room, acting the part of a college girl, being mindful of the time and the place—would all that stuff really result in hair, makeup, and clothing choices turning out *this* similar? Managing it to this degree without prior consultation sure felt like some sort of superpower at play.

"In which case, this case might be the other way around."

"Meaning?"

"If this is Adolescence Syndrome, the cause isn't Uzuki Hirokawa, but all the other college girls. The ones who *can* read a room."

Rio was dropping bombshells.

But this one made sense. Especially after using the group in back as an example—her words felt like the most logical conclusion.

"We could say this Adolescence Syndrome is unconsciously sharing information, creating a medium state of values for what counts as normal, for what everyone's doing. Or we could say the syndrome is creating an unconscious network with quantum entanglement–like properties, and the synchronization is merely a result of that."

"Affecting all college students?"

"Yep. Every single one."

This really was a heck of an idea. It boggled the mind. The scale involved was far worse than he'd imagined. But it was also true that no matter which campus you went to, there were similar student groups, dressed alike, sharing values, and acting the same.

And unlike Uzuki herself, *they* had reasons to cause Adolescence Syndrome.

Miori had told him as much.

For years, their uniforms had shaped their identities. Classrooms had given them a place to belong.

College didn't work like that. No uniforms, no classroom to call home. Everything that defined them was taken away, so without knowing it, without consciously trying for it, they all searched for ways to *be* a college student. That cluster of vague insecurities might be what Rio meant by *normal* or *everyone*.

"If that's the nature of the Adolescence Syndrome, then I can see why it would target her."

"'Cause Zukki gonna Zukki?"

Uzuki had aways been true to herself. As an idol, on TV, even in fashion magazines. To students at a loss to define themselves, that had been dazzling—and thus, something they'd rather not look at directly.

So they'd targeted her.

Dragged her in.

"From that point on, this is more your field, Azusagawa."

"Is it?"

"Statistical science analyzes this stuff, right?"

"Freshmen are just doing core curriculum and foundational mathematics."

He wasn't taking any major-specific classes yet. It didn't feel like he was doing statistics, science, or statistical science.

"But in this particular case, what we're saying here may not mean much."

"You think?"

It felt like Rio had helped change his perspective on things.

"You know what I mean," she said grimly. "If anything's gonna come of this…it hasn't yet."

"Yeah, I figured as much."

Rio was right there with him.

"When you learn to read the room…you'll figure a lot of things out," she warned.

"Good or bad."

"And you're worried that'll change her?"

"Well, isn't that what fans do?"

Kaede wasn't the only one who'd been saved by Uzuki's way of life. Her helping Kaede out had helped Sakuta by proxy. Nodoka had been right; Uzuki had a knack for bringing a smile to everyone's face. He didn't want to see a cloud pass over her light.

They were friends now, so it was natural to feel that way.

But whatever Sakuta might want, things changed.

Uzuki could read the room now.

And that meant she could see things she hadn't before.

Like what everyone around had thought of her when she couldn't.

"Make sure you aren't caught cheating," Rio said. It was unclear if that was a joke or not. Her eyes were on the wall clock; they'd already been here an hour. It was 10:20.

"Kaede's taking long enough."

She'd said to wait for her so they could walk home together, but she'd yet to emerge from the changing room.

"I'll poke my head in the back room. You go on home, Futaba."

"Oh? Okay."

Rio dropped her share of the check on the table, said, "See you at work," and left the restaurant.

Once she was gone, Sakuta called the manager over and settled the bill.

Then he headed into the back room, searching for Kaede.

As he passed the kitchen counter, he heard voices in the staff room. Both speakers were girls he knew.

He poked his head in and found exactly what he'd expected. Kaede and Tomoe, still in their server uniforms. They were both staring at Kaede's phone.

"Are you *still* not changed?"

"Oh, senpai!" Tomoe said, looking up.

"Sakuta, look! Uzuki's being amazing."

"Mm?"

He didn't know what that could mean. Uzuki was certainly on his mind, but Kaede didn't know anything about that.

"Hurry up and look!"

"I'm the one trying to get *you* to hurry up," he grumbled. They couldn't go home until she changed.

"It's legitimately amazing!"

She shoved the phone in his face, forcing him to look.

It was the wireless headphone commercial Takumi had shown him.

A young woman singing a cappella, covering a Touko Kirishima song. The ad had generated a bunch of buzz.

And since they only showed her lips, everyone was wondering just who the singer was. Takumi had told him as much.

Hiding her face certainly made you curious.

Sakuta had wondered about it himself.

If the camera had panned just a bit higher—but that commercial had ended before it did. This one was a full thirty seconds longer.

And the song hit the last chorus.

The singer's voice soared, transcendent.

The camera panned from her chest to her neck to her lips—and as the song ended, they could at last make out her face.

The sweat on her brow.

Cheeks flushed with passion.

A triumphant smile that Sakuta had seen before.

The one he had seen that day on campus.

That was unmistakably Uzuki.

"They just released the extended cut today! And it's already got a million views!"

Kaede was positively giddy. It certainly seemed impressive, but Sakuta wasn't really sure *how* impressive.

More than the number of views, the commercial's direction and the beauty and strength of her voice got under his skin. There was power radiating off the screen, and not one that could be described with mere logic.

Sakuta was clearly not the only one who'd felt that way. The video was flooded with comments.

This is the ditzy girl from all those game shows, right?

I didn't even know she sang.

This makes her look hot.

God damn.

That's what real singing is!

Zukki's era has arrived!

Some knew who Uzuki was; some didn't.

But this commercial had made everyone want to know more.

And those roiling emotions had a real heat to them—the kind that made things happen.

5

The night came and went, and it was Thursday, October 6.

On his way to college, Sakuta changed to the Keikyu Line at Yokohama Station and bumped into Uzuki on the red train. Not in the flesh or anything—just her photo hanging from the ceiling ads.

She was all on her own on the cover of a *shounen* manga magazine. She was sitting down, one leg pulled up against her chest. An oversize sweater fell off one shoulder while her black hair spilled over her pale bared skin—it was oddly alluring. But she was biting into an orange, and her expression looked rather surprised—which was cute in an age-appropriate way. Like you were seeing the real her, a face only her boyfriend would normally get to see.

Sakuta thought it was quite a photo. He decided to pick up a copy for Kaede on the way home.

He was still staring on it, thinking all that, when a voice behind him said, "Sakuta, you're staring too hard!"

He turned his head and found a girl in a mask and a hat.

The real Uzuki.

"I guess the real one's better," he said, turning to face her.

But this one had her shoulders covered. No skin anywhere. A severe lack of allure.

"On second thought, I prefer the other one."

He looked back at the poster. Honed by all that dancing, her skin had a healthy glow, sexy in a way he could stare at all day.

"Y-you're not allowed!" Uzuki squeaked, pulling his arm to turn him around.

This wasn't her typical reaction. He'd shown up with a magazine featuring her in a swimsuit once, and she'd just been excited, asking what he thought.

But if she was gonna be all embarrassed, that made him feel like he was doing something wrong. That just made him want to tease her more, but he didn't want Nodoka getting wind of that, so he let her spin him around.

They had plenty to talk about.

"You're on a roll," he said.

"Yep, counting my blessings."

"I saw that commercial."

"It even reached *you*?!"

Her voice got real quiet.

"Kaede was making a fuss about it last night. Sounds like it's a hit."

"Apparently. My manager called me this morning, saying I should be careful on my way to school."

Uzuki normally didn't hide her face at all, but today she was fully incognito.

The disguise was apparently working; nobody around them seemed to have spotted her. But quite a few had their eyes glued to the poster above them. The response to the recent commercial was strong.

Two high school girls were chatting by the door.

"That's her, right? From yesterday?"

"Oh, the commercial!"

"Yeah, yeah. What's her name?"

"Wait, I'll look it up."

They both took out their phones.

The old Uzuki likely would have gone over to them and introduced herself. Oblivious to how shaken they'd be. She'd probably have insisted on an enthusiastic handshake, too. But the new Uzuki didn't budge.

She just stood bolt upright, looking tense.

"Right, Uzuki Hirokawa."

"Is this true? It says she's going to the Yokohama city college."

"Then she might take this train!"

"Wow, we might actually run into her!"

Uzuki didn't seem to know how to handle any of this.

But an announcement came over the loudspeaker, cutting them off. The next stop was Kamiooka.

"Wanna get off next stop? Maybe switch to another car?" he suggested.

Uzuki didn't understand at first, but a moment later, she caught his drift. Her eyes went wide, then she nodded.

Sakuta and Uzuki hopped off the car at Kamiooka, but the next car *also* had high schoolers talking about her commercial. Three boys, this time.

"Her voice is so good!"

"And she's cute."

"You gonna buy that magazine?"

"You first."

It was way too early for that energy. Horny energy.

They ended up getting off again at the next stop, Kanazawa-bunko Station, before moving to a third car.

"It's like a secret date," Uzuki said, grinning. But Sakuta was Mai's boyfriend, and their current situation was mildly nerve-racking.

Regardless of his true reasons, if he was spotted with Uzuki now, people would think he was her boyfriend, and all kinds of bullshit stories would circulate. He really wasn't up to facing accusations of two-timing.

Once they finally reached Kanazawa-hakkei Station, he let out a sigh of relief without even realizing it.

They passed the gates and went down the stairs to the west exit.

Almost everyone walking this way was in college. Or faculty.

"That's some impact," he said.

The night before, he had not expected it to change things this much.

"Yeah," Uzuki said, agreeing with his consternation but not looking all that thrown by it. Why would she be? This was just another success stemming from the career she'd built. She'd finally gotten a chance to make her popularity explode, so that would mostly feel like a good thing. Train rides might become a tad more difficult, but she'd live.

"It's a one-way trip to Koshien."

"That's baseball, Sakuta."

"The Japan National Stadium?"

"That's soccer."

"Hanazono?"

"Rugby."

"Ah, then it must be Ryogoku."

"So close, but that one's sumo."

Uzuki nailed every single reference, fully aware he was doing a bit. She matched his timing perfectly. The old Uzuki would have just asked, "Why Koshien?" and made things awkward for him. How many times had she made him explain his own jokes?

"I'm trying to get to the Budokan," she added. Well aware he knew that.

"Is it getting any closer?"

"That's a good question," she said, straightening up. With the mask on, subtle expressions were hard to catch, but her tone of voice and the way her eyes stared straight ahead made it clear she wasn't going easy on anything.

Sakuta wasn't exactly caught up on the inner workings of the idol industry, but her attitude showed just what a big deal the Budokan was. At the very least, it wasn't the kind of place Uzuki currently felt like promising she'd get to, even in jest. She was picking her words carefully.

"Why Budokan anyway?"

"As long as we had a goal, I didn't mind where it was."

"Oh?"

"I told you before, right?"

"What?"

"How I stopped making friends in junior high."

"Yeah."

"So everyone in Sweet Bullet meant a lot to me. More than friends."

Only Uzuki could know how important they were. So Sakuta said nothing. He had no right to say he understood.

"Aika and Matsuri may have graduated, but the rest…Nodoka, Yae, Ranko, and Hotaru. I still want to go there with them. Together."

The last word was a whisper. Which made it clear that was what really mattered here.

And the success of this commercial would put the wind in their sails, hopefully helping them achieve their goal. It wasn't just another step—it was three or four.

But from a different perspective, her agency was already thinking about giving Uzuki a solo debut, and this could be the start of making that happen. After all, that commercial was all her.

If you were gonna make a move, it was best to strike while the iron was hot.

Just walking with her like this made it clear how much the world's eye was on her right now. The students around them were giving them lots of looks and pretending not to notice.

Uzuki was well aware of their attention and was doing her best not to look his way.

"Half of these are for you," she said.

"What?"

"The looks."

Looks of envy, wondering how he came to know not just Mai Sakurajima, but also Uzuki Hirokawa.

"But I'm glad we met."

"I appreciate your candor, but I'm afraid my heart belongs to Mai."

"Hopes dashed! I didn't mean 'met at all'—I meant 'bumped into each other on the train today.'"

Obviously, he knew exactly what she meant. And if Sakuta knew it, then she knew he knew it. And in full knowledge of that, she'd gone along with the joke and laboriously explained the whole thing.

"Sakuta, you are an incorrigible tease."

"You only just worked that out?"

"Yeah. I had absolutely no idea."

They passed through the main gates.

As they followed the path through the trees, they drew even more looks.

This was the break between first and second periods. Between the students arriving for second period and students moving between classes, there were crowds of people.

If this were anywhere else, hardly anyone would have spotted her. But everyone here *knew*. It was common knowledge Uzuki Hirokawa was a student here.

And if you were aware you might spot her on campus, then it was easier to see through her disguise. The mask and hat weren't really doing much here.

"Maybe I'll add some glasses tomorrow."

"Mai said it helps if you change up your hair."

"Oh! Good idea."

Uzuki was still staring straight ahead, as if the attention wasn't fazing her. But she knew exactly what was going on. She could feel it in the air.

Then her eyes darted to the side of the gingko path.

To an area filled with boards listing canceled classes, syllabus information, etc. A girl was standing in front of a board covered in club recruitment posters, calling out to students passing by.

"Interested in being a student volunteer?"

Sakuta knew her.

It was Ikumi Akagi.

"We only just started out, and we're eager for more members."

She was holding out flyers, but no one was taking them.

A pair of girls passed right in front of her, busy chatting. A man wearing wireless headphones raised a hand, rejecting the offer.

"We're supporting the education of children who refuse to attend school, and we still need more help."

Ikumi's voice was calm and clear, undaunted.

But not a single student stopped to talk. A few shot her puzzled frowns, but they exchanged glances once they passed her, smiling and whispering, "Volunteering, huh?"

Their eyes were saying, "Wow," or "Couldn't be me," taking stock of each other's values.

And once they'd done that—they were satisfied. They never even looked at Ikumi again. The conversation shifted right back to cafés with hot waiters or whatever.

No one else even slowed down or showed any interest.

Ikumi kept on talking—until someone finally stopped.

The girl next to him.

Not because Ikumi had spoken to her.

They were still a good ten paces away.

But Uzuki had stopped and was staring at Ikumi.

And at the crowd passing her by.

He could tell she was looking at the little smiles on their faces.

Uzuki's lips quivered. The edges of her eyes turned down. A hint of sadness.

"Sakuta…"

"……"

He waited for her to speak again.

Pretty sure he knew what was coming.

He'd thought this might come.

It was an exchange he'd hoped to avoid.

But Uzuki wasn't about to let him off the hook.

Once she'd realized, she had to ask.

Her mask was off, and she was looking right at him.

"They laughed at me, too?" she asked.

Her expression didn't change.

And he had no words for her.

Only the tiniest of nods. Barely one at all.

Chapter
3
social world

1

"A star in Orion, it will likely end in a super—"

Before the question even ended, Uzuki hit the buzzer. The light on her seat turned on.

"Yes, Zukki?" the fortysomething male celebrity running the quiz said.

"Betelgeuse!" she said, extremely confident.

There was a brief pause, then a bell rang—she was right.

"The full question was 'A star in Orion, it will likely end in a super-nova explosion,'" explained the young female announcer working as a program assistant.

"What's got into you today, Zukki?" the MC asked, overplaying the surprise. His eyes were bugging out.

She'd gotten three answers right in a row. No mistakes. She was famous for blurting out the weirdest things, so the MC's shock was likely genuine.

"I've been in great form these days!"

"But it ain't good for the show. I'm scared for our ratings!"

"I'm gonna get them *all* right!" she crowed.

"Please don't," he wailed.

All on the TV screen.

——*"They laughed at me, too?"*

Ten whole days had passed since she'd asked the question.

Now it was Monday, October 17.

He wasn't sure when this game show had filmed. But since they mentioned her commercial, it was definitely after the expanded cut was released.

The exact date aside, Uzuki's new attitude was definitely helping her reach the right answer.

"Zukki, you gonna be a real singer now?" the MC asked, joking around.

"I already am!" Uzuki said, playing the crowd and getting a big laugh.

"It's like I don't even know you!" This was no longer a performance. He looked genuinely baffled. "But I guess this is working, too, so…let's roll with it!"

Nodoka was also on the show, forcing a smile. The camera briefly cut to her, and Sakuta caught the tension she was hiding.

He couldn't be sure exactly how she felt about all this, but undoubtedly thoughts were being had. Thoughts about the changes in Uzuki.

Sakuta was watching this unfold in the staff room at the cram school.

His math classes had wrapped up, and he was writing notes on how Kenta Yamada and Juri Yoshiwa were progressing when the principal switched on the TV over the couch in back.

"This Uzuki Hirokawa's pretty funny," the principal said.

"Yep."

The game show was team based, and Uzuki's side won. The one-hundred-thousand-yen bonus challenge sadly ended in failure, and the show wrapped up.

"See you next week!" the MC yelled, and the twenty-odd panelists all waved.

Letting that play over his ears, Sakuta finished his report.

By the time he looked back at the screen, a new show was starting.

Had Uzuki's discovery changed everything? Of course not.

Sakuta and the world at large were going about their business. At the very least, the last ten days had passed without incident.

Uzuki herself had been going about life like she always did. When she wasn't working, she was in class, joining her friends, fitting right in, and laughing with the crowd. ·

She'd been in Spanish class with him today, and he'd detected no obvious changes in her.

And after what Rio had said, the way the students around them were all dressing the same and acting alike—that seemed far less natural. If this really was a case of Adolescence Syndrome affecting all college students, that was vaguely terrifying.

Sakuta was dressed exactly like the boy sitting in front of him, so perhaps he'd gotten caught up in it without even realizing. Unconsciously absorbing what everyone was doing, what passed for normal. Unwittingly allowing that to taint him.

"You were staring at Uzuki the whole class," Miori said. "Wandering heart?"

"What did you make of Zukki today?" He figured it couldn't hurt to ask.

"She seemed normal enough?" was all he got back.

Sakuta was the one asking a weird question, so he deserved that look.

But he found it hard to believe nothing was different.

Uzuki had figured it out.

She knew what her friends had thought of the old her.

She knew what the world had made of a semi-successful idol.

And that must have changed something inside her. Yet Uzuki was going about her business like everything was the same. Hanging out with the college friends who'd mocked her behind her back, eating lunch together, enjoying the good times.

It was hard for him to read that as a happily-ever-after scenario.

He didn't think this would work out long-term. If they could keep this up without anyone forcing themselves, then fine, but it was clear that Uzuki's hard work was the only thing keeping it all above water.

And the more she bottled stuff up, the bigger the explosion to come.

But knowing that alone did not give him any way to stop it. Thus, he'd spent the last ten days stewing.

"I'm outta here," he said, getting up.

"See you at your next class, Azusagawa-sensei."

"I'll be there."

Sakuta headed for the changing room, shuffling off his uniform coat. He stuck it in his locker and grabbed his backpack.

"Time I went home."

There was nothing left to do here. His fretting about Uzuki's issues wasn't gonna change a thing, either. All he could do was wait for something to happen and do what he could when it did.

But outside the locker room, he ran into Kenta on *his* way out.

"Yo, Sakuta-sensei. Have a good one," the kid said.

"Go straight home."

"Can't. I gotta hit the store and get me some of that chicken."

The kid was honest if nothing else. Kenta didn't even slow down—he was out the door already.

"Good-bye, Sensei."

This time it was Juri's turn.

"Go straight home," he said again.

"I will," she said, clearly meaning it.

She turned once at the door, bowed, and left the building.

Maybe the whole athlete culture drilled it into her, but she really minded her manners, and that made her seem older than she was. The exact opposite of Kenta.

"Guess I'd better get going myself."

But if he left now, he'd probably run into both his students in the elevator. That would be awkward, so he spent a minute pointlessly inspecting the mock exam posters on the wall.

Once he'd wasted enough time, Sakuta took the elevator to the first floor.

He scanned the road outside the office tower, but Kenta and Juri were long gone. Kenta had that chicken to buy, and Juri had probably gone straight home like kids should.

He'd avoided them, but he ran into someone else he knew.

"Oh, senpai."

Tomoe.

"Koga. Leaving work?"

The restaurant they both worked at was down this same street. She was in her high school uniform, so she'd likely had a shift right after classes ended.

"You too?" she asked, glancing up at the cram school sign.

"Yep."

He started walking toward the station, and she fell in step.

"Something wrong?" she asked, frowning at him.

"Could be."

"Coulda woulda shoulda."

"Is that a whole thing right now?"

"……?"

Tomoe just blinked at him.

"Forget it. Why'd you ask?"

"You usually go, 'Oh, it's *you*, Koga,' like you aren't happy to see me."

"Do I?" he asked, feigning ignorance.

He'd definitely had stuff on his mind, but Tomoe had always been perceptive like this.

"Fight with Sakurajima?"

"Clear sailing on that front, don't worry."

"I wasn't."

They reached the station and took the pedestrian overpass to avoid a wait at the light. It was a big one going across the whole bus terminal. The total width was a solid eleven yards, so it was less a bridge and more an elevated square.

In one corner, he spotted a young man busking. He was around twenty, Sakuta's age.

His back was to the railing as he strummed an acoustic guitar. Sakuta didn't recognize the song. Maybe the man had written it himself. There were CDs in the guitar case that looked self-printed. Probably for sale.

It was past nine, but still plenty of people were passing through the area, business types and students alike. Everyone was trying to get home, so the crowd moved fast and smooth.

The only people stopping to listen were a couple in the uniform of Nodoka's old school and a pair of girls in some other high school uniform.

Most people never even glanced his way, just passed right on by.

Everyone knew he was there. Sakuta was still on the far side of the overpass but could hear the man singing loud and clear.

"Koga," he said, slowing to a standstill, his eyes on the busker.

"What?" Tomoe asked, pausing a second later. She followed his gaze.

"What do you make of him?"

"Like how?"

Sakuta leaned back on the rail, and she frowned up at him.

"What do you want me to say here?"

She'd caught enough of his drift to look displeased.

"Your honest opinion."

Tomoe thought about it.

"I think he's something else," she said, choosing her words with care.

"In what way?"

That statement could contain multitudes.

It could be admiration.

Or it could be disparaging.

"Both ways," she said, like she was loath to admit it. She sure looked annoyed that he'd forced it out of her.

She turned her back on the busker, leaning her elbows on the railing.

"He's got a goal in mind and the drive to work for it. That much, I admire."

"Yeah."

Finding something worth working toward and actually doing so—that alone was enough to dazzle anyone just going through the motions of a life. But the light within them also provoked another kind of emotion—a shadow on the heart.

"And because I admire it, I always look away, pretending I don't see them. I blow right past, barely even realizing that's what I'm doing."

Tomoe's eyes dropped to the taillights of the cars passing below.

"If I were with friends, someone'd probably go, 'I've never heard *that* song,' and we'd all laugh."

"Not uncommon at all."

That was simply what the vast majority of people were doing. Everyone passing by knew he was there, but it meant nothing to them. And they were all thinking, *He's not that great* or *I can't make out the words* or *So cringe* or *Why bother?*

He'd seen the same phenomenon last week on campus. Ikumi Akagi earnestly trying to recruit volunteers with the crowd streaming past. To Sakuta's knowledge, Uzuki had been the only person who bothered to take a flyer from her.

"And even though they just walked right on by, if he gets famous years from now and shows up on the New Year's pageant, they'll all boast that they knew him when he was a street musician."

That was Laplace's demon speaking, all right.

Already thinking of a future that might not even come to pass.

But that side of Tomoe was what had made him ask. He'd figured she'd give him the answer he was looking for, and she'd done even better.

"Oh, but if we're talking about famous people we know, then Sakurajima wins hands down."

This must have got too real for her, because Tomoe started joking around. The mood lightened instantly.

"Well, she is my Mai."

"Riiight."

That agreement was halfhearted at best.

"But was that the answer you wanted?" she asked, shifting gears again.

"Straight-A answer. You always come through, Koga."

"That sure doesn't *feel* like a compliment."

She puffed her cheeks out at him.

"It is one. Trust me."

This only seemed to deepen her suspicions. People who said "Trust me" were almost always untrustworthy.

But at this point, a mischievous voice called out, "Tomoe-senpai!" and someone threw their arms around her.

"Eeek!"

Tomoe's squeal of surprise sounded genuine.

Several suits and students stopped to see what the commotion was. The girl hugging Tomoe wore a Minegahara uniform. She was a bit taller than Tomoe, shoulder-length hair curled out at the ends.

No one had the courage to stare at two schoolgirls hugging for long, so people quickly went back to minding their own business.

Only Sakuta was still looking.

"Himeji?" Tomoe said, craning her head.

Only then did the new girl let go.

"Just left cram school. You had a work shift?"

Sakuta knew this girl, too. The Minegahara first-year Kenta had a one-sided crush on. Sara Himeji.

"Yep, just left."

Sara's eyes shifted sideways, looking at Sakuta.

"Oh, she's…," Tomoe began.

"Sara Himeji," Sara said, talking over her.

"'Sup," he said, figuring it was best to act like he didn't know her. Explaining why he did would likely be a headache. That whole preempted-student/teacher-romance thing was best never mentioned again. And keeping his source on that name secret would be better for Kenta.

"And this is, uh—" Tomoe tried to introduce him, too.

"Azusagawa-sensei, right?" Sara said, jumping in again.

"Oh, right. He works at your cram school."

The word *sensei* provided all the pieces Tomoe needed.

"You don't take my classes, so I'm surprised you knew that," he said.

There were quite a few part-time teachers like Sakuta, and most people would never learn all their names. There was nothing to be gained by it.

"I'm in the market for a math teacher," she said.

That made sense. Especially since that was *why* he'd learned her name.

"There's this boy in my class, Yamada—you know him?"

"I teach him, yeah."

"He said you were real good at teaching, so I was thinking that might be a good fit."

She grinned at him, a twinkle in her eye. She was serious when it mattered, but she clearly had a sense of humor, too.

"I didn't know Yamada thought that highly of me."

Maybe Kenta thought if he recommended Sakuta, he'd get to take classes with Sara. That seemed likely. But this was less a cunning ploy than just hopelessness.

"Can I ask for you?" she asked.

Sara's eyes were locked on him. Staring him right in the eye. She had been the whole time. Like someone told her when she was a kid to look at people when she talked to them, and she was diligently following that advice to this day.

"If you really want to understand the math, I'd say Futaba-sensei's better. She's mostly physics but does math, too. If you just wanna pass the tests, I'm more your speed."

His unvarnished assessment got a giggle out of her.

"Azusagawa-sensei's pretty funny, huh?" she said, glancing at Tomoe.

"Maybe, but mostly he's just a weirdo."

Tomoe wasn't playing nice.

"Koga, you're bad for business."

"You weren't exactly selling yourself."

That was almost an outright attack. Sakuta had intended that as an accurate assessment. Most students cared more about their test scores than actual comprehension! At least, Sakuta had.

Sara looked from Sakuta to Tomoe, then said, "Sorry, I'm interrupting here! I'll leave you to it."

"Huh? Argh, wait…!" Tomoe tried to stop her, but she was already running off. "We're not!"

This desperate cry never reached Sara. She was already lost in the crowd.

"Tough break, Tomoe-senpai."

She hit him with her fiercest glare.

"If you see Himeji at work, make sure you untangle that mess, Azusagawa-sensei."

"If I can remember."

"You'd better!"

"Still, she super likes you."

"We were both on the sports festival committee. So…"

"Hmm."

"What's that for?"

"Seems like you're not that into her."

Tomoe had definitely been way less familiar. None of the warmth she used with her friend Nana Yoneyama.

"I don't not like her. But, like—I remade myself for high school, right?" Her confidence was slipping away.

"And she seems like she was on the ball in junior high?" he asked.

Possibly even earlier. One of those girls at the center of the class even in grade school. He'd had the same impression.

"While I was a total dork."

Scowling, she started walking. The street musician had put his guitar away, apparently done for the day.

Sakuta glanced at him once, then followed Tomoe.

"Senpai, you're actually a good teacher?"

"I spent last year studying my ass off. These are the dividends."

"You were even studying on breaks at work."

"Oh yeah, Koga, you know what you're doing yet?"

She'd said something about a girls' school in the city having referrals available.

"I managed to land a referral. Put the application in last week."

"Congrats."

"I ain't in yet."

"Referrals are practically guaranteed."

"So I hear, but you never know."

"Results announced in late November?"

"Why do *you* know?"

That just came with the cram-school-teacher territory. His students weren't sitting exams this year, but he'd heard plenty of chatter and wound up picking up stuff.

"I'm expecting presents when I get in."

"Like what?"

"Wait, you'll actually get me something? Then I know just the thing."

"What?"

"The earphones from Zukki's commercial."

They were passing the electronics store by the station's north exit. Tomoe's eyes were on the store entrance. Like he should buy them here. This was unmistakably the place to buy earphones if he was shopping local—nearly all the electronics in his house came from here.

"They're not cheap."

They were the latest wireless earbuds.

"Like twenty thousand?"

"Even worse than I thought."

"It'll help make up for everything."

"What did I do?"

"Years of sexual harassment."

She might have a point there.

"If this clears the slate, maybe it's worth it."

"Dang, I shoulda asked for something pricier."

"Let me off with Zukki earphones."

"You're serious?"

He knew perfectly well she'd been joking.

"You've helped Kaede quite a bit."

Kaede had gotten the hang of waiting tables, but at first she'd only managed it when Sakuta was also on duty. But their schedules didn't always line up, so Tomoe had done her best to take shifts with Kaede whenever he couldn't. And that had brought the two of them together.

"Guess I'm not surprised you know Zukki," he said.

"Kaede told me all about her. How nice she'd been, how fun her shows were. These days, I'm even hearing her name at school."

"Huh."

That really drove home how much buzz there was.

"She's at your college?"

A loaded question.

"Same major, so I guess we're friends."

He certainly thought they were.

"You sure know a *lot* of cute girls," Tomoe said, rolling her eyes.

"You're one of 'em."

"That's not how I meant it!"

He felt like he'd done this same bit recently. Was that with Miori? Probably.

"I'm leaving!"

Tomoe stalked off down the stairs, fuming.

"I'll walk you there."

They'd be going the same way until they were over this bridge anyway.

She grumbled at him for a few more minutes, but when she was finished with that, she started peppering him with questions about school. "Is college fun?" "Fun how?" "Did you have trouble making friends?" When that was done, he saw her off and headed on home.

2

The next day, Sakuta left the house on his way to college and found Nodoka out front. Hat pulled low, eyes downcast, her back against the wall by the entrance. She saw him step off the elevator, and the look on her face was definitely "Finally!"

This was no chance encounter. She had clearly been waiting for him.

"No Mai?" he asked, coming closer.

"Her shoot ran late, so she crashed at a hotel and is going straight to class."

She seemed in unusually low spirits.

"I know—she called last night."

They'd mostly talked about plans for Saturday. Mai had a rare day off and suggested they go somewhere together. But Sakuta had a shift at the restaurant until three and couldn't get out of it. They'd ultimately agreed to meet near Fujisawa Station once he got off. Mai had mentioned a movie she wanted to see, so they'd likely end up one station over, at the Tsujido movie theater.

"Then don't ask."

Nodoka was definitely being unusually downbeat. Less hostile than...dead on her feet.

It was just past nine, and he had a second-period class at ten thirty.

He wasn't sure what Nodoka wanted with him, but he didn't want to miss his train, so he started walking. She matched his pace.

It was a ten-minute walk to Fujisawa Station. At this hour, people with regular jobs or school were all done with their commutes, so traffic was light. No crowds to push through.

Not far from the apartment building, they passed the park where he'd once traded butt kicks with a high school girl. And from that point on, it was a gentle downslope.

Nodoka didn't say much at first, but halfway down this hill, she blurted, "I got a favor to ask, Sakuta."

"If it's Mai, I'm on it. We'll make a happy home together."

"I'm not asking about *that*."

Even this lacked her usual spark.

"Then what? Zukki?"

"……"

His abrupt swing left her momentarily speechless, but she recovered fast enough.

"Yeah. This is about Uzuki," she admitted. "We had dance practice yesterday."

We was Sweet Bullet in this case.

"And?"

"Everyone else was out on other jobs, so it was just me and Uzuki."

She broke off, like an idea hit her.

"Did I say we've got a pair of concerts this weekend?"

"Kaede told me."

Saturday was a joint concert with other idol groups. Sunday was an outdoor music event on Hakkei Island.

Kaede wanted to go to both, but Kotomi Kano wasn't available on Saturday, so she'd abandoned the idea. She and Kotomi were both going to the Sunday event, and she was excited about it.

"I know I always say this, but if she calls me, I can hook her up with tickets."

"Kaede's a Zukki stan and doesn't wanna rub that in."

"That *does* sting."

Her glare suggested she blamed him.

"So what happened at rehearsal?" he asked, ignoring her.

Nodoka didn't look pleased, but she got back to the point. "The dance teacher got pissed off at her. That never happens—like, legit the first time ever."

"Why?"

"Like, she just wasn't focused. Out of it the whole time."

"So…?"

"So I got worried and asked if she was doing okay."

"And?"

"She blew me off with a fake smile. 'I'm fine, sorry. Got myself an earful!'"

Nodoka was keeping her voice flat, but that just drove home how big a deal that was.

"Whoa, that is serious."

"I know, right? Uzuki always shared *everything*."

The back half was a whisper, like it wasn't for him. She looked wistful.

"And that's got you all depressed."

She'd been in the dumps since they met up. Clearly, this was why.

"I don't know what's going on with her."

"You used to?"

That was itself an accomplishment.

"…Well, no, but that's not what I meant."

"I know."

Previously, her unpredictable behavior had mystified everyone.

But now she was consciously hiding how she felt. The nature of the mystery was fundamentally different. Diametrically opposed, even.

"Online, they think she's gearing up to leave Sweet Bullet."

"Yeah?"

That was news to him.

They got caught at a red light, so Nodoka took her phone out of her purse. She tapped the screen several times, then showed it to him.

There was a site collating idol news.

It didn't exactly give sources, but there were articles with headlines like "Uzuki Hirokawa's Graduation Imminent?!" or "Zukki's Solo Debut Incoming!"

"That commercial sure has the office in an uproar. I asked the chief manager and was told to focus on our next concert. Pfft."

"Like admitting there's stuff they can't talk about."

"Yep."

"And you're connecting that to her performance in rehearsal."

Her mind had been elsewhere. But *where*? On leaving the group? On a solo debut? Or on something else entirely?

Nodoka was staring grimly up at the red light. There was no way she was thinking about anything besides Uzuki's potential exit. But the sadness in her eyes was likely more because Uzuki had refused to confide in her.

Whether the rumors were true or not, if she heard the news from Uzuki, Nodoka would probably accept it. Part of her wanted what was best for her friend. But instead, Uzuki had given her a phony smile. And that had left Nodoka high and dry, unable to press the point further.

"So what do you want from me?"

"If Uzuki's in trouble, help her out."

Nodoka just laid it out there, not mincing words at all.

"That's it?"

"I mean, if you can pry anything out of her, then do that."

"I gotta interrogate her?"

"God no."

She looked genuinely mad at that one. Her eyes said, "Don't push your luck." If he kept cracking jokes, she might actually kick him. Sakuta didn't see the point in inviting violence, so he took the hint.

The light turned green, and he fled her scary stare.

"Are you even listening?"

"I'll do what I can. But I can't do what I can't, so don't get your hopes up."

"Mm. Thanks."

That seemed like it took a load off. She looked way less tense.

At Fujisawa Station, they boarded the Tokaido Line and exited at Yokohama Station. The train into the city was still fairly packed, even at this hour.

For that reason, they didn't talk much, just minded their own business.

Once they'd switched to the Keikyu Line, they were outbound, and the vibe was much more relaxed.

The express for Misakiguchi raced along, skipping most stations.

Sakuta and Nodoka were hanging on to straps, jostled by each bump, talking about the school festival next month. Apparently, there was a beauty contest.

"Holding one of those with Mai around sounds like hell on earth."

"The male side of the competition allows entry by proxy. Should I put you in?"

"I don't wanna get any more popular, so I'll pass."

At that point, the train pulled into Kanazawa-hakkei Station.

The doors opened, and he followed Nodoka out.

As he did, he thought he recognized someone's back out of the corner of his eye.

He caught a glimpse through the doors between cars.

In the car ahead of theirs, Uzuki stood on the side away from the open doors.

He could see her face reflected in the glass.

The bell rang, warning that the train was leaving.

Before the doors closed, he jumped back on.

"Sakuta...?" Nodoka asked, spinning around. She looked surprised and confused.

But the doors slammed before he could explain. He just pointed at the car ahead.

Looking even more confused, she glanced that way—and hopefully spotted Uzuki, but before he could be sure, the train pulled out, leaving Nodoka behind.

Smartphones sure did help with moments like this, but Sakuta didn't have one.

With no means of contacting her, he gave up and settled into an empty seat.

He glanced up at the map above the door. The express stopped at Oppama Station, then both Shioiri and Yokosuka-chuo Station. After that, it stopped at Horinouchi and turned into the Kurihama Line. From the point, it stopped at everything until the tracks ended.

Where was Uzuki going?

She was still leaning against the door, vacantly watching the view go by. It didn't seem like she'd simply missed her stop.

Uzuki didn't get off at any stations on the way.

Half an hour after leaving Kanazawa-hakkei, they reached the end of the line—Misakiguchi Station.

Sakuta did consider getting up and speaking to her, but he wanted to see what she was up to, and he wound up leaving her to it.

The doors opened, and the few remaining passengers disembarked. The man across from him pulled a fishing kit off the rack, slung a cooler over his shoulder, and said, "All right!"

Even with the train empty, Uzuki didn't move.

Was she gonna ride it back to college?

But then she seemed to realize it was the end of the line, looked around, and got off...like she had nothing better to do.

Sakuta followed her out.

She was about five yards away, her back to him.

Tailing her any farther would be creepy. Objectively speaking, anyone following a college girl idol around was bad news. So he elected to call out to her.

"Skipping school, Zukki?"

Her shoulders quivered. Then she turned slowly around, frowning. When she saw Sakuta, she blinked in surprise. She didn't ask why he was here. She could probably imagine why, or maybe she simply didn't care.

"I was in the mood to...to find myself," Uzuki said, as if that was a joke. It didn't sound like one.

"You do that at Misakiguchi?"

"I dunno. What's around here?"

"I think they have tuna."

He glanced at the station sign. They were so hype on tuna here they'd even made the sign say Misaki Maguro instead.

"Welp, I'm pretty hungry. Wanna go have some tuna and think?"

It was eleven now. A bit early, but arguably lunchtime.

3

An hour and a half after they got off the train at Misakiguchi, Sakuta somehow found himself following Uzuki's butt around. A well-toned butt hugged by the elasticity of her skinny slacks. More accurately, her butt was on a bike she was pedaling, and he was following on a bike of his own.

They'd been at this for half an hour now.

How had things gone so wrong?

Everything had been reasonable when they left the station.

They'd found a roundabout outside backed by skies of that autumn blue. No tall buildings anywhere, so it felt wide-open.

A view that promised a relaxing escape from the daily grind.

The tuna they were after didn't take long to locate. There were flags fluttering across the roundabout with *maguro* written on them.

The sort of shop that served meals by day and booze at night.

It was small but comfy.

Sakuta and Uzuki ordered the tricolor tuna bowl. Akami from a bigeye tuna, *otoro* from a southern bluefin, and Pacific bluefin *negitoro*. Everything was heaped on top of the rice, all fancy-like. It came with miso and a side for 1,300 yen, a real bargain. And with Misaki Harbor close by, it was as fresh as it was affordable.

Personally, Sakuta would have been satisfied pigging out and going home. Sadly, Uzuki was still searching for herself and didn't find it in the tuna bowl.

They settled the bill and went outside.

"Now what?"

He figured she didn't exactly have a plan, so he wasn't expecting much of an answer.

"Let's rent some bicycles!" Uzuki cried.

"Where at?"

"The tourism guide booth by the station exit."

She'd kept her eyes peeled while he'd been gaping at the skies.

They headed back across the street, and there was a bike-rentals sign on the door of the tourism counter.

"You can't find yourself without a bicycle."

"I don't think they're usually rented."

She paid this advice no heed, opening the door and calling out, "Excuse me!"

The clerk inside was super nice and walked them through the paperwork, even recommending a good route to take. They got a map of bike paths in the Miura Peninsula area.

Since then, they'd been pedaling around for half an hour now. Possibly a full hour.

At first, there had been cars around, plus homes, and warehouses dotting the landscape. Now there were fields to the left, to the right, and dead ahead.

No people anywhere.

Aside from the occasional farmer toiling in those fields, they didn't see a soul.

"What leaves are those?" Uzuki asked.

"Daikon. Miura daikon."

They were still growing, so only the green leaves were sticking out of the soil. If you looked close, you could see the bulbous white top of the root.

"You know so much!"

"We took a field trip to a daikon field in grade school."

He had not expected to avail himself of that education here.

"So, Zukki…"

"Whaaat?"

"How far we going?"

"Dunno!"

She sure sounded carefree.

"Which way we going?"

"The sea!"

Simple enough.

"What happened to the map?"

"The guide said not to look while we're riding!"

"True…"

Nothing he said was getting through. But today, Uzuki felt more like the one he knew, and that was oddly comforting.

And even if they did get lost, her phone had GPS, and they could find their way back. They'd come a long way, so he was a bit concerned about their energy reserves, but these bikes were actually pedelecs, so going uphill was not that bad. Quite breezy, really.

"This feels great!" Uzuki cried.

She had a point. Their impromptu bike tour of Miura Peninsula was surprisingly enjoyable. The breeze was pleasant, the skies were clear, and the air was the right kind of dry.

And they had the road through the daikon fields all to themselves.

"*Nodoka*, right?"

"What about Toyohama?"

"Not her! The meaning of her name! *Tranquil!*"

Uzuki let out a peal of laughter. The autumn wind carried it to him.

"I've been wondering…"

"Mm?"

"Why'd you pick this major, Zukki?"

He'd been wanting to ask that for a while now but never quite had the right opportunity.

There were plenty of options. She could have joined Nodoka over in the international liberal arts school. Or maybe made like Miori and majored in international management.

"Why'd you go with statistical science, Sakuta?"

She turned the question back on him.

"Seemed like the least competitive division."

"Then I'll go with that, too!"

"C'mon!"

"You lied, so I'm not telling."

She laughed out loud again. Her general demeanor and enthusiasm were definitely the old Uzuki, but she was still reading him loud and clear. She knew exactly how he felt and what lay behind his words.

"I wasn't lying!"

"But it's not the truth, either."

"......"

She had him there.

"Oh, the sea!"

She waved excitedly, one hand off the handle bars. Pointing ahead.

"Careful. Eyes front!" he said.

Uzuki slowed to a stop.

They'd crested a long, gentle slope.

Sakuta pulled up alongside her and put his stand down.

"Let's take a break," Uzuki said, stretching.

Her back had been bolt upright the whole ride, so she must've been feeling pretty stiff. She ran through a number of stretches, clearly ones she did all the time. When she touched her shoes, her forehead tapped her knees. Then she twisted hard, bent backward, stretched her legs out to the side, and even pulled them up to her head.

Since she was wearing skinny slacks, this left little to the imagination, but her figure was so relentlessly healthy it didn't really prompt bad thoughts. And the view around them was hardly fitting for that kind of fantasizing.

A college idol stretching against sea, skies, and daikon fields.

Not a sight you saw every day. Sakuta took a swig of tea from a bottle he'd bought from a vending machine along the way. He'd looked for a brand from one of Mai's commercials, but they hadn't had any. He'd been forced to compromise.

"Can I have a sip?"

"It'll be an indirect smooch," he warned, handing the bottle over.

She pulled her hands away.

"I'll stick to mine, then."

She'd bought some water at the same machine and took a few gulps from that.

As he watched her, she asked, "Did Nodoka put ideas in your head?"

She wasn't looking at him.

"Mm?" he said, as if he had no idea what she meant.

Uzuki smiled faintly. Like she'd seen that answer coming. Her eyes locked on the road through the daikon fields, to the sea beneath the distant skies.

The wind brushed by.

The daikon leaves shivered.

Thin clouds trailed across the sky.

A moment passed, almost without sound.

"Sakuta."

"Mm?" he grunted, midswig.

"How old do you think idols get?"

"You'll manage it your whole life."

He put the cap back on his bottle.

"I said that once."

"But not now?"

"I dunno."

She smiled faintly, her eyes never leaving the water.

"Where's this coming from?"

"A friend at school said something."

"What?"

"'How long are you gonna do that idol *thing*?'"

"And that made you wonder?"

"Nope. I thought something else."

"And that is?"

"Just 'cause you had a fight with your boyfriend, don't take it out on me."

"Brutal."

It was so harsh he couldn't help but laugh. That was definitely not something the old Uzuki would have come out with. She would never have picked up on the aggression in the first place.

"People don't say that stuff, but they think it all the time, right?"

Looking down on idols.

"Everyone wants to be something," Sakuta said, his eyes on the ocean, speaking absentmindedly.

"To be what?"

"Something they can boast about. 'This is me!'"

"……"

"Hirokawa, in your case, that's singing. The whole idol shebang."

And people admire that.

It's something to brag about.

Everyone wants something like that.

"……"

Uzuki said nothing back. Just gazed at the water, listening.

"But they ain't anything yet. So when they see you on TV, living the idol dream…well, that's downright bedazzling."

And they lack the strength and aplomb to admit that to themselves. Sometimes it turns into irritation, and they find themselves sneering, "How long are you gonna do that idol *thing*?" That results in pure vindictive spite because they realize they have *nothing* of their own.

A standard-issue self-defense instinct.

"Well, my friend does have a point," Uzuki said, ducking Sakuta's words. She smiled at the empty scenery. "You can't be an idol forever."

"Hmph."

"Hmph? Ain't that where you're supposed to argue I can?"

"Do you want encouragement?"

"If you gave me any, I'd get real grumpy."

"Then I should have gone for it."

"Why?"

"'Cause if you blow your top, maybe you'll finally start saying what you mean."

Like Uzuki's friend had.

"…You can be a real bully."

"Not really."

"You're good at pretending you are and getting people to blurt stuff out."

"Like…?"

"Like how we're a *long* way from the Budokan."

She said that like she wasn't speaking to him. Almost as if they weren't even her own words. The wind caught her voice and carried it away. But this felt like the truest thing she'd said yet.

She only let herself express it in that detached tone—but failed to disguise the bitterness behind the words.

And knowing where that came from made it all fall into place. Sakuta realized why Uzuki had needed to go out and find herself.

She didn't think they could do it.

Didn't think they'd get there.

Didn't think they had it in them.

Didn't think her comrades' hard work would ever make their dreams come true.

She thought they were doomed to failure. And the realization that she thought that way had dawned on her.

So she'd gone out looking for something. Anything to distract herself from the truth.

"Zukki, lemme borrow your phone."

"Why?" she asked, but she also handed it over.

First, he fired up a train navigation app. Looking up the obvious.

"It's actually pretty close. Only a two-hour ride from Misakiguchi Station."

"To where?"

"Where else…? The Budokan."

"……"

Uzuki went real rigid, like she rejected the very idea with her entire body.

But that didn't last long.

She managed an awkward smile.

"…I knew you were a bully."

Sakuta handed the phone back and got back on his bike. He took a firm grip on his handlebars, making a show of being ready.

"This whole bike tour thing was fun, but you didn't lose yourself out here, Zukki."

"Are you suuure?"

She didn't sound convinced, but she did get back on her bike.

"Still...Sakuta!"

"Mm?"

"We've gotta get back to the station first."

Unfortunately, neither of them knew which way to go. That was a pretty tall order.

4

"Okay, that was far."

Behold, the Budokan.

It had taken them a solid three-hours to make the trip, and Sakuta's mutter was steeped in all manner of regret. The long journey had left him aching all over. His body screamed in agony, primarily caused by all that pedaling. Getting back to the station had taken more out of him than anticipated.

"I told you so," Uzuki said with a wince, resting next to him. All those intense dance lessons had her fit as a fiddle, and she didn't look the least bit tired.

Bathed in the streetlights, she looked ready to go another round.

They were well into fall, and past six, the skies were dark.

In the dim glow of the streetlights, the Nippon Budokan definitely cut an imposing figure.

In the open space by the entrance, the wind rustled through the multicolored leaves.

It felt like the air here was extra clean.

Almost like when you step onto the grounds of a shrine. Equal parts still and somber.

There didn't seem to be anything happening here tonight, and the area was hushed.

A few people were cutting across the square, but only Sakuta and Uzuki had stopped to stare up at the building.

"What do you think?"

"……"

Uzuki clasped her hands together behind her back, staring up at her dream manifest. For a while she said nothing, just blinked occasionally. From her profile, Sakuta could not discern her thoughts. So he said nothing and waited for her to speak.

"Sakuta."

"Mm?"

"Do you know how many idol groups stand on this stage every year?"

"Nope."

Not only did he not know, it had never occurred to him to look it up. At best, he had the vague impression that lots of idols or musicians made that their goal. Even though the name itself suggested it was not primarily a concert venue.

"At most, five groups make their debut here a year. Some years, not even one."

"...Ah."

That number didn't really mean much to him one way or another. But from the way she picked her words, he could tell only a select few were ever allowed to stand on that stage.

"And there's thousands of idol groups in Japan now."

She spoke like that was just some unrelated little fun fact.

"I dunno if all of them are seriously trying to get here, though."

But five out of a thousand was certainly not a lot. Clearly an extremely low number.

"And where are you ranked, Zukki?"

"Sweet Bullet's about thirty right now."

"That sounds pretty good."

He was legitimately impressed.

"Not really," Uzuki said, shaking her head.

"Yeah?"

Even if it wasn't good enough to secure them a spot on that stage, Sakuta thought "thirty" sounded like it symbolized a lot of potential. But Uzuki seemed to feel the opposite.

"We're on TV, they know our faces, people spot us on the street— but all we can fill is two-thousand-seat venues."

Uzuki looked up at the Budokan.

"How many does this seat?" he asked.

"Ten thousand."

She placed no weight on that number. It was just a statement of fact. Ten thousand minus two thousand was a whopping eight thousand.

Sakuta didn't really know how big a gulf that eight thousand fans was. What he did know was far more basic.

"But you knew that from the get-go?"

"...Yeah, I did. I knew that when we made this our goal. I knew, but I forget it along the way."

Her eyes dropped to the ground a few yards out.

"Is this really where I wanted to go?"

"......"

Sakuta didn't have an answer to that. Only she could know, and it was something she'd have to make up her own mind about.

"I never used to worry about these things."

"Would you rather go back to not reading the room?"

He threw that question out, and Uzuki didn't overreact. She just kept her head down and shook her head.

As clear a sign as any.

Uzuki was well aware of how she'd changed.

Sakuta didn't know when that had happened. He didn't have an exact date or time. But in this moment, she clearly did know.

"I'm glad I learned how. I mean, I finally get your sarcasm now."

Reading the room allowed her to crack jokes like that.

"And you can tell when your friends are being snide."

"See, *that's* what I'm talking about!" she laughed. "You're so mean!"

"Well, gotta live up to my rep as an incorrigible tease."

That earned him a wince.

"And now that I get these things, I know what my college friends actually mean when they say I'm 'amazing.' A lot of things a lot of people said have taken on new meanings."

Uzuki looked up, gazing into the distance. The Budokan was still in front of her, but it felt like she was looking right through it. Or maybe not looking at anything at all.

"Like, there's all these people in my head saying stuff, and if I listen to all of them, then I don't know who I am anymore."

She smiled, like she was laughing at herself. This was something the old Uzuki had never done.

"……"

When Sakuta said nothing back, her smile faded.

"Sorry," she said. "What am I even talking about, right?"

Now she was trying to laugh off what she'd just said.

"I get it," he said, not letting her wriggle out.

"……"

"I get what you're saying."

"Really?"

She seemed unconvinced and faintly taken aback.

"If you know how other people feel, that changes how *you* feel."

That had happened to Sakuta.

When he'd made his beloved Mai cry, that had really gotten to him.

When he'd realized what was going through Shouko's head, he could barely stand it.

And to his mind, both of those emotions had been unquestionably genuine.

No matter how much thought he'd put into an answer, a single moment could change it.

Being with other people changed him.

Contact with others let him discover new sides of himself.

"The 'self' is less defined than you'd think. Nobody really knows who they are."

"Maybe you're right."

These days, other people's feelings and moods rush indiscriminately through phone screens. Even if you aren't looking for it, information overload is everywhere, and there are endless sources of things influencing people.

You might not wanna know. You might not wanna see. But once you knew, once you saw—it was too late.

You can't go back to not knowing.

That knowledge makes a new you.

And you have to live with yourself.

Out of nowhere, Uzuki had learned to read the room. A huge quantity of information and people's feelings had flooded her senses. She never noticed her friend's snide remarks before, but now she was all too aware. She'd learned the difference between what people say and what they think, between what they show and what lies within. And a world based around those discrepancies was hardly appealing.

But she still said she was glad it had happened. And while marking the difference between her own interior and exterior—she'd smiled.

"Think this is Adolescence Syndrome?" she asked, looking right at him.

The question caught him by surprise, but he did not need to look for an answer.

"Probably."

"If it's cured, will I go back?"

"Probably."

"That would be *rough*."

He got why she'd say that.

——"*They laughed at me, too?*"

That one phrase said it all.

She didn't want to go back to not knowing when people made fun of her. That's why she'd kept hanging out with those friends, enjoying their conversations. Eating lunch with them. That was the normal life she'd obtained now that she could read the room. But she'd also started to doubt herself, which was why she'd skipped school today.

"Which me did you like better, Sakuta?"

"I like both."

"But you do have a preference."

"I like both."

This time, he put a bit more emphasis on the *both*.

That got a hint of a smile from her.

"I'd say the new me has more fun talking to you."

"Sorry I was such a bore."

"I mean, the witty repartee just doesn't stop."

Just like she claimed, Uzuki was visibly enjoying herself. And Sakuta could hardly object to that. There was definitely a kind of banter he could only do with her now, and he was undeniably having fun.

"Anyway, talking with you sure helped clear my mind," she said, stretching.

He found it hard to believe this had cleared much of anything.

"Thanks for keeping me company."

Her tone got weirdly formal, and she made a show of bowing.

When she straightened up, there was a bashful smile on her face.

It was definitely the best-looking fake smile he'd ever seen.

"……"

And that made it impossible for him to leave well enough alone.

"Sakuta? What's up?" she asked, pretending she didn't know.

They'd spent all day together, but he still hadn't moved even one step closer to the heart of the matter.

What had she been searching for in Misakiguchi?

What had she been trying to find at the Budokan? He really wasn't sure.

Had Uzuki really been searching for herself? He didn't even know *that*.

But she wasn't fleeing reality. Her presence here proved that. If she was, this would be the last place she'd want to be.

As he mulled this over, a buzzing interrupted his thoughts.

Uzuki's cell phone.

She pulled it out and glanced at the screen.

"It's Nodoka."

She looked him right in the eye and made a face. Then she put the phone to her ear.

"Hello?" she said, mega-cheery. "Sorry, I'm late for rehearsal, right?"

Apparently, they were still doing prep for the concerts that weekend.

"Now? Um, I'm still in the city, so I'll rush right over to the studio."

Nodoka must have asked where she was. Uzuki had wisely elected not to say, "The Budokan."

"I should be there in thirty! Mm… Huh? Oh, yeah, he is. Hang on."

With that, she held her phone out toward him.

"Mm?"

"Nodoka said to put you on."

"……"

He silently took it from her. He expected Nodoka would give him an earful, but he wanted to talk to her anyway. What he'd heard from Uzuki had left him with a favor to ask.

"Toyohama? Got a question for you."

Sakuta decided to steal the initiative.

"Huh? I should be the one asking the questions!"

"Can we still get tickets for the concert Saturday?"

He straight up ignored her complaints.

"Aren't you going out with Mai?"

News spread fast.

"Yeah, and I'm thinking a concert would be a good date."

He'd have to ask Mai what she thought, but she likely wouldn't object.

"…Hang on."

Nodoka left the receiver. He could hear her whispering, probably checking with someone. After a twenty-second silence, she said, "I can get two people on the list."

"Noice. Then put us on."

"Sure. But…is Uzuki that bad?"

Her voice got real quiet.

"I dunno."

He wasn't expecting anything to go down onstage.

Uzuki was a lot better at hiding her feelings, and that left him without much insight. He just figured it was worth attending.

"Just hook us up."

"Got it. Bye."

Nodoka hung up on him.

He turned to give the phone back and found Uzuki looking at the moon in the night sky. It wasn't quite full, but close enough.

"There's no rabbit up there," she murmured.

"Probably for the best. No air *or* food."

Sakuta held out the phone, and she took it from him.

"Where's the fun in *that*?" Uzuki chuckled.

Chapter

4

idol song

1

His shift at the restaurant over, Sakuta left the shop to find the skies cloudy. Maybe coming from that typhoon that had been hanging over the Ogasawara Islands all week. Currently, it was headed north and not slowing down. But the weather report predicted it would turn into an extratropical cyclone before it hit the mainland and pass over the waters south of Kanto early next week. It would probably not get too bad here.

But that didn't mean there were no effects. October was half-over, but the air had returned to midsummer levels of humidity.

He was going to be out and about with Mai today, but the weather was not cooperating.

It was 3:10, and they were meeting up in five.

Mai had said to meet in front of the restaurant he worked at, so all he had to do was step outside, and he was there.

Figuring she'd be coming from the station, he looked that way and took a few steps down the road from the entrance.

It was almost three fifteen now. Still no sign of Mai. She was big on punctuality and almost never late. But Sakuta saw no one coming who looked like her. She wasn't showing up in the nick of time here; this was legitimately tardy.

What could he pry out of her by way of apology?

His heart filled with hope, he squinted at the station again, and a car from the opposite direction pulled up beside him.

"……?"

It was almost like this ride was here *for* him. Puzzled, he turned toward it.

A two-tone vehicle. The body was white, but the window frames and roof were black. The fenders and side mirrors were black, too, and the whole thing had rounded curves. It looked kinda like a panda.

The car was a compact made by a German company, the design had made it quite popular, and he saw it about town often enough. This model had five doors, including the luggage space.

The door opened, and someone stepped out of the driver's seat.

"Get in," a voice came across the roof. Unmistakably Mai's.

"Um…Mai?" he said, unsure where to begin.

"Hurry up."

She sat back down in the driver's seat without waiting for a response.

He had infinite questions, but she was clearly in a hurry, so he clambered into the passenger seat. It was roomier than it looked.

"I'm in."

"Seat belt?"

"On."

"Then let's head out."

Her hands on the wheel, Mai checked her mirrors. She waited for a car to pass, then turned on her blinker and eased on the gas.

The car quietly pulled out. It gradually sped up, moving away from the restaurant. Soon, the roof of the building was out of sight.

They drove straight down the road, his cram school passing in the blink of an eye. By the time he turned to look, it was already gone.

He glanced sideways at Mai. She looked completely comfortable behind that wheel. She had fake glasses on, her hair loosely bound and falling down her front. It left the nape of her neck bare, which was always sexy.

"Um, Mai?"

"What?"

She kept her eyes front.

"What is this?"

"A car. Heard of them?"

Of course he had.

"You bought one?"

This was less a question than a confirmation. Mai was *the* Mai Sakurajima, so buying a car hardly counted as a major expense. She'd bought herself a condo while still in high school...making this a comparatively trivial purchase.

"Just before summer vacation. But then I was away on shoots, so I had them hold off on delivering it."

"Your license?"

"I have one, obviously."

Driving without one *was* illegal.

They got caught at a light just after Fujisawa Station, so she reached into her purse, pulled out her wallet, and showed him her license.

It certainly said *Mai Sakurajima* on it, with her Fujisawa address listed. The genuine article. And of course, it had a picture of her to go with it. ID photos have a distinct tendency to turn out awful, but Mai's looked just like the Mai Sakurajima. Astonishing.

Come to think of it, her student ID photo had also been totally Mai Sakurajima. Was there a trick to it? Or did it just come down to superior raw material? Probably both, so he decided not to ask. It was no skin off his nose if his student ID photo featured dead fish eyes. He could always get a laugh from showing it to people. Spread some good cheer in the world.

"So when'd you get it?"

"Last year, while I was shooting the morning soap. Hit up the driver's school around that schedule."

Fall to spring, then.

"If you had time to spare, you could have gone on more dates with me."

"You were too busy studying, and you know it."

So this was his fault now?

"You had no time for me, so I was forced to get a license to keep myself occupied."

And yet she'd still done her part to tutor him. Impressive.

"Sigh…"

"What was that for?"

"I was planning on taking lessons myself, once I'd saved up a bit."

"Don't let me stop you."

"Get my license in secret, then surprise you with a driving date."

He'd figured that might let him spend a bit more time with someone as famous as her. She was good at going unnoticed, but her office were being extra careful lately, and most of her travel time was now in her manager's van.

"Well, I did the exact same thing," Mai said, smirking.

"You got a license to take me on a date?"

"Exactly. A car makes it much easier to go out."

"And not because you needed it on a shoot?"

"Well, that, too."

"I thought so."

"Stop grumbling and navigate."

"Where to?"

"Odaiba. We're seeing this concert, right?"

As he started giving directions, Mai turned on the stereo and played Sweet Bullet songs to set the mood.

2

Mai made a few detours on the way to the concert venue, and they got stuck in a few patches of congestion, but they made it to Odaiba just past five, as the sun began to set.

She'd certainly given Sakuta a fright when she said, "I heard you and Hirokawa went on a date?" but being alone with Mai in a closed car was a novel experience, and he enjoyed every second.

"We just went to Misakiguchi, ate some tuna, and rode bikes around the daikon fields."

"That's what we call a date."

He made excuses but had been thinking the same thing the whole day, so he changed the subject as soon as possible.

Traffic had picked up around Odaiba, but by five thirty, they managed to find a parking garage with vacancies and drop the car off.

By the time they got out of the garage, it was 5:40.

The concert itself was supposed to start at six. The gates were already open, and the lobby was likely packed with fans desperate to see their favorite idols.

Sakuta and Mai were in no hurry, and they took their time walking along the sidewalk.

They had always planned to slip in at the last second, avoiding attention. The roads had been more crowded than anticipated, but arguably that meant they'd arrived right on schedule.

It being Saturday, Odaiba was filled with pleasure-seekers. The crowd definitely leaned young. Lots of twenty- and thirtysomethings. And many foreign tourists.

Mai was walking next to him. She'd swapped her fake glasses for a hat and mask. She'd worn a cute sweater in the car, but now she had on a baggy jacket, hiding a figure the envy of women everywhere. Neither her expression nor silhouette was anything like the Mai Sakurajima everyone knew. Perhaps for ease of driving, she was wearing skinny slacks down below—so this look really emphasized her long, slender legs, baggy jacket or no. Even in disguise, Mai always managed to project an aura of beauty.

As they crossed a busy intersection, Mai put her arm round Sakuta's, her fingers lightly resting just above his elbow.

"So you don't get lost," she explained.

"I don't have a phone, so don't you dare let go."

It was crowded enough that they had trouble not bumping the pedestrians crossing in the other direction. If he lost Mai here, it was all over.

"You been here before, Sakuta?"

"Nope. Never had a reason to."

So he didn't really know where they were going.

Mai seemed to be moving with purpose, so he was following her lead.

"You come here often?"

There was a TV station nearby, so he could see why she'd know the lay of the land.

"Not often, but occasionally. Mostly for work."

Soon enough, he spotted a large shopping mall up ahead. There was a giant robot standing out front that looked like it was over twenty yards tall. Parts of it were glowing red. Sakuta couldn't help but gawk.

DiverCity Odaiba didn't mess around. This place had everything. A regular cornucopia.

"It transforms," Mai said.

"Seriously?"

That sounded worth seeing, but Mai didn't even slow down. She pulled him past the robot to the concert venue beyond.

Inside, Mai spotted the reception for staff and friends.

"Go on," she said, letting go.

"Me?"

"Didn't Nodoka tell you there'd be two tickets under *Azusagawa*?"

"She did not."

Putting the tickets under *Mai Sakurajima* would likely attract unwanted attention.

Sakuta headed over, and a woman in a suit asked, "May I have your name, please?"

"Azusagawa."

She checked the list on her table and found his name right away. He could tell from the look in her eyes.

"Here's two tickets. Head right on in."

"Thanks."

"You're welcome."

He left the desk and rejoined Mai, and they headed farther in.

Down a short passage, they opened the soundproof doors and were in the concert hall itself.

The standing area was already packed to the brim. Even at the back, there was no elbow room. This was still less than two thousand?

They moved along the back wall, finding a tiny pocket to occupy. And as they did, an announcer started reading the rules.

No recording, no climbing onstage, don't bother those around you, get hype but not too hype, etc.

This concert was a joint one, with four different idol groups performing three or four numbers each. Sweet Bullet was the second group on. He'd heard a man near the reception—likely another concertgoer—say he'd heard there was a secret guest, so there might be one last group.

But the secretest guest was likely Mai herself.

"Any moment now," she said, checking the time on her phone.

A second later, music started pounding, and the first group ran out onstage.

"Let's go, Odaiba!"

Six girls in all, dressed all in black, their music rough and powerful.

Not all idol groups were cute, clean-cut, and poppy. There were groups leaning into rock, metal, or punk styles.

Uzuki had said there were thousands of idol groups out there. While many followed the major trends, it stood to reason there'd be some that bucked the vogue. That kind of competition helped create new things and the trends of the future.

Not everyone in the industry had what it took to be the next Mai Sakurajima. Mainstream superstars like her were far and few between.

Sakuta turned to look at her, and she picked up on his attention, looking back at him, her eyes asking, "What?" He shook his head, indicating nothing. She rolled her eyes with a laugh.

Nothing special about that back-and-forth, but it was a happy moment nonetheless.

The first group sang three songs.

Their fans were yelling the names of members, and their cheers reached the stage. The girls waved back and then dashed off.

Once the stage was clear—the lights turned off. Intentionally.

"Ooooh!"

The audience's anticipation was like a low rumble rising from below.

A moment later, a soft glow lit the stage. The vacant space now filled with the five members of Sweet Bullet, their backs turned to the crowd.

One at a time, they turned around, singing a brief solo. The last to turn was the girl in the center—Uzuki. The song had started with an arrangement of the chorus, but now the main musical riff soared out high.

The fans' voices echoed over the intro. "Zukki!" "Doka!" "Yanyan!" "Ranran!" "Hotarun!"

But they didn't want to ruin the song itself, so when the main melody kicked in, they stuck to waving glow sticks, moving with the music just below the stage itself.

The group was boosted by their fans, though it was Uzuki who pulled the group's vocals along.

Her voice caught each note and captured the emotion behind each lyric, and the rest of the girls followed her lead. She was the core of the act, and it was her performance that brought the song together. Even at concert volume, five voices in harmony felt oddly comfortable.

It had been a solid year since Sakuta had been to a Sweet Bullet concert. During summer the year before, some family business had made Kotomi Kano drop out last minute, and Kaede had forced her ticket into his hands. He hadn't been back since.

It was clear they'd made dramatic improvements.

All of them were better singers now.

They could really belt it out.

Their choreography had always been polished, but it was even more unified now. From the tallest to the shortest member, all movements were as one, in sync.

That level of polish really caught the eye. It was hard to look away.

Even audience members here for the other groups were sucked in. He could see jaws dropping around him.

But even with this level of magnetism, Uzuki had said they were a long way from the Budokan. They needed five times the fans they had right now.

What more could they do?

He didn't think Sweet Bullet's performance power was in any way inferior. They had the skills, so why was their growth stymied? Sakuta was hardly the one to find the answer. If the solution was so easy to figure out, they would've already solved it and been onstage at the Budokan now.

As these thoughts were running through his head…

…Sweet Bullet's flawless concert started to unravel.

At first, it was minor, almost like he was imagining it.

But it felt like Uzuki's dancing alone was lagging slightly behind.

Maybe that was the intent.

It only became obvious when Uzuki and Nodoka swapped positions. Nodoka's eyes momentarily looked concerned.

He checked Mai out, and she was frowning.

Something was wrong.

The fans were starting to pick up on it, and the glow sticks grew unsteady.

All eyes turned to Uzuki.

Uzuki kept dancing slightly off the beat, her eyes staring into the distance. Her smile didn't fade, but she wasn't looking at the fans.

Sakuta was getting real concerned.

He didn't know what was going on.

He didn't know *if* anything was about to go down.

But at the least, he felt this was objectively not something that could be put down as "in bad form today."

And that instinct proved right.

As they hit the second chorus, it happened.

Uzuki's voice broke, like the words caught in her throat.

Her mic caught a rasp. Almost like a grunt of pain.

But Sweet Bullet's song didn't stop. Nodoka and the other members took over Uzuki's solo.

Uzuki was in the middle of them, still holding her mic and singing. But it didn't look like her mic was picking up any sound.

"Audio problems?" Mai whispered. But she was clearly worried about something *else*. The same thing he was.

The first number ended.

All members of Sweet Bullet were facing the crowd in a row.

"Hello, everybody!" Yae Anou said, like nothing was wrong. As expected of the group's subleader, she easily took command.

"We're—"

"—Sweet Bullet!"

All members cried as one. But the microphones only picked up four voices.

Uzuki's was not among them.

She moved her lips, but Sakuta couldn't make out a thing. He likely wouldn't have even if he'd been right up front.

Possibly because she was aware of the problem, Yae kept the patter brief, saying, "We're short on time, so let's get back to the music! We've got two more songs for you!"

Before the next song began, everyone but Uzuki exchanged quick glances.

There was a lot of meaning packed behind each look, a testament to how much time they'd spent together.

Sweet Bullet got through their second and third numbers without major incident.

Like during the first song, Uzuki alone was slightly out of step and clearly just moving her lips—but they showed no signs of canceling the performance.

The whole time they were onstage, they were all bright and shiny like idols should be, smiling away.

As they ran off, the third group took the stage, not letting the hype die down.

Before their first song began, Mai said, "Let's go."

And Sakuta followed her out to the hall.

Little noise made it past the soundproof doors. It was like a different world out here.

Like they were back in reality.

They left the building and walked toward the parking garage.

As they crossed the first light, Sakuta forced himself to speak.

"Mai, was that…?"

"I think her voice died."

He'd wondered as much.

"I doubt we'll get a reply soon, but I'll text Nodoka," she said, and she stepped off the main path. Sakuta stood next to her, Mai's words echoing through his mind.

——*"I think her voice died."*

He wondered what that meant to someone who sang.

3

Nodoka's response arrived an hour later.

We're at the hospital.

A short text to Mai's phone.

It sounded like the second they left the stage, they'd taken Uzuki to a doctor.

Mai asked where, saying she'd pick her up, and it turned out the hospital was close to Odaiba.

By the time Sakuta and Mai reached the hospital, it was eight thirty PM.

The lot was almost empty. Mai put the parking brake on, and they took off their seat belts. They opened their doors and stepped out.

"Is that the right entrance?" Mai asked.

Outpatient hours were over. The back entrance had a red light out for emergency patients, and that was the only passage that seemed to have lights on. Figuring they could go in elsewhere if the staff said to, they headed toward it.

And on the way, they ran into a couple of familiar faces.

Uzuki, with a bench coat around her shoulders. She was still in her stage costume and hadn't even removed her makeup. Almost like she'd just shed the jewelry and run straight here.

By her side was her mom—Sakuta had met her once, a while back. She'd been a teen when she'd had Uzuki and hadn't quite left her thirties behind—she definitely didn't look like she had a daughter in college.

They both saw Sakuta and Mai coming.

"Sakuta! Long time no see," the mom called. "And Mai."

They both bobbed their heads. Then turned to Uzuki.

"You okay there, Zukki?" Sakuta asked.

"……"

She didn't answer. Just smiled awkwardly.

"Sorry, her voice just isn't working right now," her mom said, not changing her tone at all.

"……"

"……"

That left Sakuta and Mai speechless.

Mai had called it.

Her voice really had died.

In the car on the way here, Mai had told him a few stories about people with these symptoms. Too much stress or bad news from work that left them temporarily unable to speak, no matter how they tried. She'd seen people lose their hearing or suddenly start slurring their speech, too.

He didn't find this hard to believe because he'd lived through the memory loss Kaede's dissociative disorder had given her.

Human emotions and bodies are more entwined than most people think.

"We've been told to get some rest for now. She *has* been busy," Uzuki's mom said. "Well, probably not as much as *you*, Mai."

Uzuki looked like she had something to say but...couldn't. Her mouth kept opening and closing.

Sakuta was watching her do this, and she noticed, meeting his eye. She managed a smile and quickly looked away.

"If you're here for Nodoka, she's still inside, talking to the manager. About tomorrow."

Sweet Bullet had a Sunday concert, too. That would require contingency plans.

Uzuki's mom pulled her car keys out of her jacket pocket. The lights on a minivan behind them flashed.

"Hate to run, but I'm gonna get her home."

"Take care."

What else could he say?

Uzuki gave him a little wave, bobbed her head in Mai's direction, and slid into the passenger seat. Her mom made sure her belt was on, then waved to them and drove away.

The van quietly pulled out of the hospital lot.

Half the lights in the hospital halls were off, and it was rather gloomy. There was no one around. Sakuta's and Mai's footsteps echoed.

The hall went on for a while, but when they turned the corner, it got much brighter.

They heard voices.

"So you *are* talking about having Uzuki go solo?"

The speaker sounded pissed. Was that Nodoka?

They stopped, peering ahead. Five figures stood before the internal medicine outpatient desk. They were in a little meeting area, but none of them had taken a seat.

The Sweet Bullet members were all wearing the same bench coats as Uzuki. Nodoka Toyohama, Yae Anou, Ranko Nakagou, and Hotaru Okazaki. All four sets of eyes on an adult woman facing them.

"Nodoka's manager," Mai whispered.

She looked to be around thirty. She wore a well-cut suit jacket and glasses that made her look intelligent and collected. She definitely wasn't having the best day, but she didn't seem defensive.

"Well?" Yae said.

"You gotta tell us!" Hotaru said. She had kind of a baby voice.

"Manager!" The last plea came from Ranko, the most grown-up-looking member.

"...Fine," the manager said, throwing up her hands. "The chief said to keep it quiet, but it's true. There's talk of having her go solo."

"Would that mean she graduates?" Hotaru demanded.

She didn't specify graduate from what, because everyone knew already, and she probably didn't want to say it out loud.

"......"

But neither side said anything further.

Had he timed it, the silence would probably have been only five seconds. But it sure felt agonizingly long.

"The chief thinks that's for the best."

"......!"

All four girls bit their lips.

"But Uzuki rejected the idea."

"......"

Nodoka looked up, frowning. She wasn't ready to celebrate.

"Why?" she asked.

"I couldn't say."

"When was this?" Yae asked.

"Right after they shot the commercial. Like...end of August?"

"That's..." Ranko gasped. She probably meant to add "so long ago"?

"At the time, the chief let it drop. But after seeing how people reacted...well, he couldn't leave well enough alone. He wants more people to see how great she is. Truth is, we've been getting offers to launch a solo career from some pretty heavy hitters."

Sakuta assumed that meant big-shot producers in the music biz.

"And you told Uzuki this?" Yae asked, making sure. It sounded like she was chewing over each bit of information, one at a time. Nodoka stood next to her, with the same look on her face, thinking hard.

"We have not. The chief said he was waiting for the right moment."

"Then why has Zukki been acting all funny?" Hotaru wondered. That question got right to the heart of the matter.

"......"

But it didn't seem like the group's members had any answers.

They'd all sensed it. They'd all noticed the change in Uzuki.

And they'd all secretly assumed this must have been about the solo career offer. But from what their manager said, that theory was off base.

But they couldn't be sure. They didn't have enough clues. What was Uzuki carrying that left her without a voice?

"What about you?" the manager asked. "Any idea what could be weighing on her?"

"......"

No one said anything. Another long silence. But this one had a very different meaning. The girls were looking at one another. And there were definitely ideas.

"I'll take that as a yes."

"......"

But still none of them spoke.

"If you don't wanna tell me, fine. Can you figure it out?"

Yae nodded, for everyone.

"Then we'll be there tomorrow, as scheduled."

""""""Yeah,"""""" all four said in unison.

"Just be ready for the worst."

Even Sakuta knew what that meant.

If Uzuki still didn't have her voice...

4

No one spoke on the drive home. There was one more passenger this time, yet silence reigned.

Hands on the wheel, Mai focused on driving. Sakuta was in the passenger seat, and Nodoka was behind him, staring out the window, watching the world go by. In the side mirror, he could see a melancholy look on her face.

For a while, the car stuck to main roads, but as they passed Yoga, Mai took the big sweeping curve onto the Daisan Keihin toll road. They passed through the electronic toll collection gate and sped up. By the time the Tama River shot by beneath them, Mai's car had merged into traffic and was going fifty miles per hour.

From there, they cruised along, covering a lot of ground.

Unable to bear the oppressive silence any longer, Sakuta popped the cap on the soda he'd bought at the convenience store just before the concert. Peach flavor.

He took a sip.

"This *is* pretty good."

"……"

"……"

Mai and Nodoka did not deign to respond.

So much for his attempt at lightening the mood. Such harsh rewards.

He was still reeling when a voice from the back seat hit him.

"In the green room before the show…"

When every other emotion was being held back, only regret remained. There was no trace of Nodoka's usual spunk in her voice. It sounded so different, for a moment Sakuta didn't even realize it was her.

He checked the mirror again, and she had her elbow propped up against the doorframe, head leaning against the glass. Her eyes were still on the scenery but likely not seeing much of anything.

"Uzuki asked us all something."

Mai said nothing.

Sakuta followed her lead, waiting.

Nodoka's next words were very quiet.

"'Do you think we can make it to the Budokan?'"

"……"

"Any other day, I'd have said, 'You know we can.' Or 'Let's make it happen.' I always have."

Nodoka's whisper was almost lost in the hum of the engine.

"It was a thing we always did. When we were upset about a gig getting canceled or we messed up on the job and lost confidence. When we threw ourselves into singing and dancing lessons but weren't seeing any increase in fans and felt like crying. When Aika and Matsuri graduated. Any time one of us felt crushed by it all, it was like our code. 'Let's reach Budokan together.' That's how we've always picked ourselves back up."

Her voice was getting choked up. Not from sadness, or loneliness, and obviously not from joy. This was regret. She was disappointed in herself. Her eyes were welling up.

"I've always said it, but today I couldn't."

"……"

"Not me, not anyone else. The words are so easy, but when Uzuki asked, no one said anything."

"……"

"And I know why. The first one to speak up was *always* Uzuki. She was always the one who pulled us all out of our moods."

It was *easy* to pile on afterward. Someone had already said it. Someone had already made the choice. The burden wasn't on them.

"Uzuki was keeping *all* of us afloat. And now she's the one who's lost…and we couldn't do anything for her."

Sakuta didn't think this was entirely true. When Uzuki's voice had died midshow, *every* Sweet Bullet member had stepped up and helped cover.

It had been a problem that could easily have derailed everything, and they'd chosen not to cancel but to finish out their set. Only they could have pulled that off.

There were definitely fans who'd noticed something was wrong. But since the show went on, they hadn't been worried. The results spoke for themselves. It was the best possible outcome given what they were dealing with.

That wasn't a stunt you could pull off on short notice. Nodoka had mentioned they were spending a lot less time together these days, but today's concert had demonstrated the depths of their power *as a group*. And the audience had been that into it *because* that came across.

But saying any of that now would mean little to her.

"I just assumed Uzuki would always be okay."

The car was still cruising along.

Mai still wasn't saying anything.

Sakuta gave her a sidelong glance, but she was just maintaining a safe distance from the white SUV up ahead.

Mai's car had taken them through Kawasaki, and they were entering the Yokohama city limits. She took an exit to the Yokohama Shindo.

The navigator screen showed they just had to pass the toll at Totsuka, then follow Route 1 all the way to Fujisawa.

For a while, they drove in silence. Finally, Mai said, "What'll you do tomorrow?"

She asked in a totally typical tone of voice. Her hands rested on the wheel, and her expression was relaxed.

Nodoka jumped at the question and peeled her face off the window. She righted her posture, her back a bit too straight.

Maybe she thought she'd be scolded for all that whining.

Mai was generally super nice, and while she didn't often say so aloud, she really did wish Nodoka every success. She always downloaded the track whenever they put out a new song, and she bought the CD, too. She'd put Sweet Bullet music on in the car on the way there today.

But the flip side of that was that she could be kinda harsh when anyone griped about the rigors of celebrity life. She was just as harsh on herself—and that was part of why she'd maintained her popularity.

Sakuta himself had shifted to the window side of his seat. He'd taken collateral damage from one of these spats before. She probably wouldn't start slapping anyone in the car, but his flight reflex had kicked in.

Mai noticed and shot him a quick glance—but said nothing.

He'd almost rather she had. The silence was scary.

"Tomorrow will be just the four of us. No Uzuki."

"Can you do it?" Mai asked.

"Yes. Obviously."

Nodoka's tone didn't sound too confident. She was still scared. They didn't know for sure they could pull this off. But she wanted to make it work, and that's why she said so.

"Okay," Mai said. A smile played about her lips.

"We can't let Uzuki go on freaking out. We've gotta keep our shit *together*."

5

When he opened the curtains, there were mountainous clouds drifting slowly from west to east.

Every now and then, a patch of blue would show itself. Was it partly cloudy or partly sunny? It could go either way.

"Which way will today's concert go?"

Sunny? Cloudy? Or would it rain? Was a storm coming?

He'd checked the weather forecast yesterday, and there'd been both a sun and a raindrop. Sunny with a chance of rain—a very summery kind of unpredictability. The man reading the report had bluntly said, "The skies might be clear, but bring an umbrella anyway—this rain might come out of nowhere."

Sakuta stared up at this indecisive sky through half-lidded eyes.

He clearly hadn't slept enough and was ready to topple back into bed.

The previous day, he'd worked a shift, met up with Mai, seen a concert, and dealt with the fallout. The hospital visit had made them come home late—but still only just past eleven, so that wasn't why he hadn't slept.

The main reason was that the second he stopped in the door, Kaede hit him with a million questions about Uzuki. "Is she okay?!" "What about tomorrow?!" "What did Nodoka say?!" She'd even talked at him through the bathroom door, so it went on for a while.

"How'd you even find out about Zukki's thing?" he asked.

Kaede hadn't been at the show.

"There's articles about it online!"

When he got out of the bath, she showed him her laptop screen. There were several articles about what went down during the show.

It was basically *all* speculation. Not a single definitive fact. And the headlines were pure clickbait, trying to rile her fans up. They'd made up a story about fighting within the group, baselessly suggested Uzuki might be graduating soon—all just stirring the pot.

Since Uzuki was in the limelight to begin with, it was easy for these articles to draw views. That's why there were so many covering the same ground. That's how these people made a living.

"She'll be fine."

"Really?"

"I mean…it's Zukki."

And she had Nodoka and the other Sweet Bullet members looking out for her. She had her fans. She'd always perked them up, and now they'd do the same for her.

So it was no use anyone else getting depressed.

"Mm, true."

Kaede must have caught his drift, so she swore to be there for Uzuki even if it rained. That didn't mean all her worries were gone, but she'd gotten what she needed for now and retired to her room.

Yawning, Sakuta rolled out to the living room—and found Kaede up and ready to head out.

It was after nine AM, and each second took them closer to ten.

"Leaving already?"

The outdoor concert started at one. The venue was on Hakkei Island, so it would only take an hour to get there. He knew she was fired up, but it was a bit *too* early.

"I'm meeting Komi at Yokohama Station, and we're getting lunch together."

With that, Kaede headed for the door.

Sakuta and Nasuno just watched her go.

"Take care!" he called.

"I will!"

The door opened, and she stepped out.

"She's grown so much," Sakuta murmured, genuinely touched.

Alone in the house, Sakuta made himself a late breakfast, did the laundry, and cleaned his room. He didn't leave until eleven thirty.

The trip from Fujisawa to Hakkei Island was almost the same as his college commute. Identical until Kanazawa-hakkei Station.

He could probably have trimmed ten minutes off it by going a different way, but this route meant most of the fare was covered by this train pass.

Even on the same train, the Sunday crowd was totally different. The vibe was super "day off." Especially once he hit the Keikyu Line—it was all couples and families with kids. They must have been headed out to Misakiguchi. Or stopping at Yokosuka-chuo Station on the way. Maybe even headed for Hakkei Island like Sakuta.

When the train reached Kanazawa-hakkei, quite a few people got off. Including a bunch of people with little kids and young couples. Through the gates, they all made a beeline for the Seaside Line.

Sakuta among them.

The Seaside Line station had originally been a short walk away, but the remodel had made transferring much easier.

Like the name suggested, the train took them on elevated tracks along the coast. This high up, it commanded a view of a wide expanse of ocean.

The windows did their work. While he gazed absently at the water, they stopped at three stations and then arrived at his destination, Hakkei Island.

Just as the stations named Enoshima weren't on Enoshima, this station wasn't actually on Hakkei Island.

He left the gates and then the station, following the crowd from his train toward the ocean.

Their eyes were trained on the island ahead and the bridge to it.

Not far now.

Sakuta walked alone, surrounded by couples and families. Mai had work and couldn't come. It was rare for her to have prolonged time off on weekends—the previous day had been an exception.

Slightly conscious of the looks he was getting, he made it safely across the Kanazawa-hakkei Bridge, reaching the man-made island beyond. With his visit to Odaiba the day before, he was spending a lot of time on reclaimed land this weekend.

The island was covered in aquariums, amusement park attractions, shopping malls, hotels, and an arena—a massive sea-themed leisure facility.

It was on TV a lot, so he'd known it existed, but this was Sakuta's first time here. When you lived close enough to go somewhere anytime, it was easy to never get around to it. In his mind, this was just one of those places.

But now that he was here, it was bigger than he'd thought.

The vibe was "well-maintained park." Or maybe theme park, specifically. Since it was October, they had Halloween decorations up, and that certainly added to the latter impression. He followed the signs to the concert venue, heading farther in.

Looking up at the tracks of a huge roller coaster, he passed through the shadow of a building, and the view opened up ahead.

He'd made it to the far side of the island. This was a square with an ocean view, and a lot of people in it.

The stage was set up on one side, and someone was already performing—he didn't recognize the name.

They were a four-man rock band.

They seemed fairly popular with the ladies—there was a passionate crowd up front.

Looked like today wasn't *all* idols.

The next act was a singer-songwriter from Kanagawa. She had a guitar and a harmonica, and her gentle melodies filled the venue with a warm fuzzy atmosphere.

The crowd was quite varied.

Fans here to see a favorite artist mingled with people who just happened to be on Hakkei Island and decided to check out the concert.

It was clear which half was more excited.

The fans were trying to get as close to the stage as possible, while the rest hung out toward the back, halfheartedly clapping. There was another set watching the stage from even farther away.

There was plenty of space to move around. Lots of people going, "There's a show on?" and giving it a listen. Sakuta was one of them.

While the enthusiasm levels differed, the crowd itself was sizable. Maybe two thousand hyped-up fans by the stage—like the show the day before.

And a solid five or six hundred non-fans.

Kaede and her friend Kotomi Kano must have been out there somewhere, but the crowd was too big to find them. This wasn't an environment suited to meeting anyone.

"Thank you, Hakkei Island!" the thirtysomething singer-songwriter said. She waved and left the stage.

She was replaced by a young woman—the MC. She approached the edge of the stage, mic in hand.

"Next up is Sweet Bullet!" she cried.

The intro music started, and the group's members ran out onstage.

Yae Anou, the subleader—she'd been throwing herself into the action on a lot of sports-themed variety shows lately.

Hotaru Okazaki, who'd been getting more TV acting jobs. She'd even had a role opposite Mai.

Behind her was Ranko Nakagou, who'd been working as a pinup model on the side.

Fourth onstage was Nodoka Toyohama, blond hair sparkling.

That was all.

There were five members in Sweet Bullet, but the fifth was not here.

The fans up front naturally spotted Uzuki Hirokawa's absence. A ripple shot through the crowd. Anxious whispers.

As if trying to blow that all away, Sweet Bullet began belting out their number.

No mention of Uzuki's absence, performing like they always did, all smiles for the fans.

High-energy, crisply choreographed routines.

Vocals that soared even on an outdoor stage.

The stage itself was a bit wide for the four of them, but that didn't mean they looked small.

And the fans responded to their energy. They yelled, clapped, and jumped with them. A few drops of rain fell, but nobody cared. It might've even heightened the energy.

They blasted through the first song without letting the hype fade.

Hair wet, drops glistening on their necks—and not all from the rain.

Panting, they paused to catch their breath.

Without anyone calling for silence, a hush settled over the crowd.

Everyone gulped, waiting to see if Sweet Bullet would address the missing member.

The only sound was the soft patter of the rain.

"Hello, everyone!" Yae cried. "We are—"

"—Sweet Bullet!"

All four voices in harmony, their standard greeting.

"Wait, aren't there supposed to be more of us?" Hotaru asked, using her baby face to full advantage.

"Er, are we going there?" Nodoka scoffed.

"It's *hard* singing Zukki's parts!" Ranko grumbled.

The crowd was laughing.

"So where *is* she?" Hotaru asked, taking the lead again.

"Look, the crowd's accepted it—just move along!" Nodoka hissed. Another laugh.

"Zukki's parts are *hard*!" Ranko said, evidently not done griping.

"I'm on half of them! I know! Yae, don't just stand there—do your thing."

Nodoka was *clearly* over this and blaming their subleader.

The whole riff felt incredibly natural. The fans came to their shows to see them banter like this.

"Don't worry," Yae said, turning to the crowd.

All eyes focused on her.

"Uzuki *will* come back to us!" she cried. "For now—we sing!"

With that, their second number cranked up.

It was one of their standards, a song that always got the crowd jumping.

With the fans' enthusiasm secured, everyone meshed perfectly with the routine onstage.

A couple from the "There's a show on?" crowd near Sakuta were whispering.

"Wow, that's crazy."

"Mm."

And wincing at each other. The idol fans were a bit too excited for them. But they weren't moving away. Their eyes stayed on the stage, interested. Curious. And they weren't the only ones.

As it went from the second verse to the chorus, the fans got even wilder. And the rain started falling harder. It was getting to the point where Sakuta wanted an umbrella.

Sakuta glanced up at the sky and saw dark clouds overhead. It had been blue skies a moment ago, and he could actually still see it in the distance. Like the weather report had said, random clouds had suddenly shown up and had brought random shifts in weather.

No telling what a few minutes from now would bring.

But once this song ended, Sweet Bullet had only one last number, and they'd be done. Their slot was only three songs long.

And this song only had the final chorus left.

They should wrap up fine.

But even as he thought that, there was a crack.

Every light onstage went out.

A wave of surprise ran through the crowd, crashing up against him.

The idols' eyes went up, glancing at the lights.

The music had stopped, too. The mics weren't picking up their voices. The speakers were dead.

Everyone got real quiet. The whole venue went still.

Electric problems? Power was dead all over the venue. The rain was the most likely cause...

...but that left the four idols stranded. Just standing there onstage.

A murmur ran across the room.

A man ran out of the wings in a staff uniform. He was holding a megaphone.

"We're looking into the issue!" he called. "Please bear with us."

He simply announced a pause in the show and then left again.

Someone ran bench coats out to the girls onstage to keep them warm. Not sure what else to do, they put them on.

This was dire.

Obviously for the fans, but also for everyone in Sweet Bullet.

They'd wanted so much to pull this concert off without Uzuki here.

That emotion had driven them onto that stage.

And having those hopes dashed like this was a serious blow.

And that's likely why they stayed onstage even when the staff urged them off. They wanted to finish. Wanted to keep going. And that kept them where they were.

But despite what they wanted, the concert was at a standstill, and part of the crowd was starting to drift away. Especially those at the back, who'd just happened across the show.

The rain was falling harder. Sakuta really wished he had an umbrella. He pulled up his hood, trying to make do.

Even the crowd at the front was starting to crumble away, wanting to get out of the rain. One or two at a time, little clusters peeling off. With no telling when the show would start back up, they must have decided to seek refuge.

And from up onstage, that was all too easy to see.

He could see the members of Sweet Bullet and their pursed lips, visibly frustrated by their lack of options.

More and more people were leaving the front of the stage. But the thinning crowd helped him spot someone in their midst.

The reason he was here today. The person he'd come here for.

Uzuki was standing there, in a gap in the crowd.

She had a baseball cap on and a hood pulled over that.

Her eyes were boring into the stage, looking more worried than anyone else present.

Sakuta had figured she'd be here. Even he'd been concerned enough about this show to make his way here—no way she'd stay home.

He moved slowly over to her and stood by her side.

"You come to these shows often?" he asked. Like he didn't know her.

"……"

Uzuki's eyes glanced his way. But with no voice, she soon turned them back to the stage.

"I won't tell anyone."

"……?"

"Even if you talk to me."

"……"

Her expression didn't change. She showed neither surprise nor confusion. Didn't insist she'd lost her voice.

This was the truth.

"You knew I was lying?"

"Liars are good at spotting other liars."

He'd first suspected at the hospital. She'd just seemed far too calm. She hadn't been at all emotional—and that had seemed unnatural. It was like she was hiding something—and in that situation, Uzuki had only one thing to hide.

"And you're a liar, Sakuta."

"Yeah, we're both weasels."

"That's mean to weasels."

"They're magnanimous creatures."

"Are they?"

Uzuki let out a little laugh, like she was trying to jump-start her feelings. Their banter trailed off, and there was a short silence.

She was the first to break it.

"I really did lose my voice during the show," she said, making excuses. "Though I suppose you won't believe that."

Uzuki shot him a nervous glance.

"I believe you. I was there."

That had not been acting. Sakuta had read that as a shock to everyone.

"You were in the back, right?"

"You saw me?"

"You can see a lot from up onstage."

"Then they've probably spotted us."

Sakuta looked up at stage, where Sweet Bullet was still gamely waiting.

"...Yeah."

Uzuki mustered an awkward smile.

The constant downpour was drenching her hoodie.

"I come to every concert."

"......?"

"Your first question."

"Oh."

"I was at the first Sweet Bullet concert, and I've never missed one, no matter how small the venue."

She spoke softly.

"Have they had problems like this before?"

He matched her pretense, acting like she was just a fan. He was the one who'd started that, after all.

"Yeah. Not on a stage this big, but they've had speakers die before."

"How'd they handle it?"

"Kept singing without mics. At least, their center did."

Even as Uzuki spoke...

...Sweet Bullet began ditching their bench coats.

The stage was pretty far from here, but he saw them make eye contact and take a deep breath in unison. A moment later, four voices rang out in harmony.

No accompaniment.

Nothing blaring through the speakers.

Their mics weren't picking up a thing, and the rain itself was getting pretty loud. The patter on clothes and pavement was very noticeable.

But the four idols lined up onstage, singing together.

Where Sakuta and Uzuki stood, they could only just make it out.

A barely audible song.

But that was enough to get the mood changing.

Someone near the front started clapping. With each clap, more people joined in, spreading backward through the crowd.

Parts of the crowd that had been on their way out stopped. Half-confused, half-curious—and they stayed put, watching the girls onstage and the fans.

It was hardly a flawless performance. They'd abandoned the idea of dancing, focusing on the song alone, making it sound more like a ballad.

The ring of applause reached Sakuta and Uzuki. A sense of unity beyond idols, fans, or any other labels.

But even this could not stop the crowd's exodus entirely. Half the audience was gone.

And more were still leaving.

Behind Sakuta and Uzuki, people were muttering.

"So she never showed up?"

"This is dumb. Let's go."

They turned and walked away. And they weren't alone. Audience members who'd just happened to be here didn't care what Sweet Bullet was going through.

They'd only stopped to watch because the girl from the commercial might show up.

And if she wasn't, they were outta here. Plain and simple.

"That's our reality," Uzuki whispered.

But she spoke loud enough that he could hear.

"They all poured their hearts out, but that's not getting ten thousand hands clapping."

There were maybe six hundred people left.

"They've got the power."

"Yeah. It was a good concert."

Nothing rang false about that line.

"Then why hang around back here? Go on up."

Uzuki's voice was working fine. She could sing, too.

"I don't have the right."

"You're a member of Sweet Bullet. Their leader. Their center."

"I'm just like them."

She clearly meant the people who'd scoffed and moved away. Sakuta looked over his shoulder, but they were long gone.

"I've got that voice in me. Part of me's laughing at them for working so hard on a dream they'll…never realize."

"……"

"And now that I know that, I can't go up there with them."

She wasn't lamenting this or openly grieving. It was just a statement of fact. Her eyes were locked on the stage, with only a hint of wistfulness.

The previous day, when she'd asked the others if they could make it to the Budokan, she'd almost certainly used this tone of voice. Distant, objectively assessing the reality.

This was the only way she could address it. Sakuta glanced at her profile, and she looked lost.

——"*They laughed at me, too?*"

She'd learned the truth that day.

If that had been all there was to it, Uzuki wouldn't be here, staring up at the stage.

There was something else she'd noticed.

She'd understood *why* people had laughed at her.

Because she'd learned to read the room.

She'd learned to recognize sarcasm and spite.

And found herself divided between what she said and what she meant, mocking others behind their backs.

But what of it?

That was just what people *do*.

Everyone feels like that.

Everyone does it.

So…

"Toyohama gets it."

"……?"

"She knows she's an unsuccessful idol."

"……"

"And she's well aware that people make fun of her for it."

But she was still up there onstage, singing her heart out.

"I bet the others do, too."

And they kept singing.

"They know that at this rate, they'll never make it to the Budokan."

"……?!"

"They know the deal."

"…So, what?" Uzuki's voice shook.

"Are you seriously asking that?"

"……"

"This one's so easy even I can figure it out."

He knew Uzuki got it. She'd spent enough time with the others, worked as hard as they had, been on the same stages. No matter how small their crowds, no matter how many people passed them by, they'd all put in the work *together*.

He figured she knew better than anyone. She should've known it in her bones.

Nobody knew how those girls onstage felt better than Uzuki herself.

"What…am I supposed to do?"

The song was entering the second chorus. There wasn't much left.

"Read the room, Zukki."

That was all Sakuta could really say.

Uzuki's head went up, and she looked at him. Faintly surprised.

Tears welled up, but she quickly wiped them away and turned back to the stage.

That was the Uzuki Hirokawa he knew.

She threw back the hood.

Tossed him her baseball cap.

Let her long hair spill down her back.

The second chorus was already over.

The audience was clapping out the vocal-less interlude, and Sweet Bullet was humming over it.

Before the final chorus was the bridge—which was always Uzuki's solo.

Even in the real version, this was a quiet beat, accompanied only by a piano.

Fans who knew Sweet Bullet's music knew to stop clapping just before the bridge began.

It was so they could focus on her voice.

A hush fell. The rain wept. Uzuki took a breath.

And her voice rang out.

Every eye in the place swung around and found her in the crowd.

The girls onstage were looking their way—at Uzuki.

She took a step forward, then another. Without anyone saying a word, the crowd before the stage parted, forming an aisle for her.

Uzuki strode down the center of it.

Singing and dancing.

As the bridge ended, she was right below the stage itself.

"Zukki!"

Four voices cried together.

"Zukki!"

The crowd called in response.

"Come on!" Yae yelled, and they put their hands together and pulled her up onstage.

A ray of light pierced the clouds. Like a ladder rolling down from above. It lit the sea, the crowd, and the stage.

Like a spotlight from heaven.

There was a screech, and the speakers came back on. Everyone realized the power was live again.

Someone handed Uzuki a spare mic, and all five gathered at the center of the stage before they sang out the final chorus together.

The fans cheered. A standing ovation.

In the center of that jubilation, Sweet Bullet shed tears…and smiled.

Last Chapter

congratulations

The sky soared far above.

The air was as clear as could be.

Lighter than blue, but too vivid to call pale.

The moon hung there, shaped like a rugby ball.

Sakuta was gazing up at it, laughing. It looked so fake.

He was on the road between Kanazawa-hakkei and the main gates of campus.

Patches of other students were all around.

The day after the outdoor concert, which had been plagued by rain and technical issues.

Since that had been a Sunday, today was inevitably Monday. And of course, classes were held like normal.

No matter what happened off campus, the college grind went on.

He passed through the gate, stifling a yawn.

The student in front of him didn't even bother.

This was pre–first period, so everyone was headed farther in. It wasn't even nine yet. No one had reason to be leaving campus.

And yet, when Sakuta looked down the ginkgo path, he saw someone walking his way.

A friend of his.

Uzuki.

She spotted him and came over.

When they met, they stopped in the middle of the path, the athletic field to one side.

"Zukki, you leaving already?"

First period hadn't even begun. Why had she even shown up?

"I stopped by the student affairs office and dropped off my withdrawal."

"……"

That was sudden. He wasn't sure what to say.

It took his brain a moment process what *withdrawal* even meant here.

"…You don't waste time."

That felt in line with her character, though. And he could guess *why*.

At the end of the previous day's concert, Uzuki had made two announcements, both to the fans and to the members of Sweet Bullet.

First, that the rumors were true—she'd been offered a solo career and accepted it. But she *wasn't* leaving Sweet Bullet. She was gonna do *both*.

And second…

"I'm gonna take *everyone* to the Budokan!"

An even bolder claim.

"So all of our fans! Nodoka, Yae, Ranko, and Hotaru! Everyone, do your part! Take *me* to the Budokan!"

Not the most orthodox way to wrap things up.

But hearing it made everyone in Sweet Bullet come in for a group hug, and the crowd went wild.

Not reading the room at all, Uzuki called for an encore, and the other girls gaped at her, but someone on staff took pity on them and started another song, so the five of them got to perform one final number together.

The concert wound up being a big success.

The a cappella third number during the power outage particularly made waves. Recordings of it were up on the Internet, and Uzuki's dramatic entrance had earned them a whole slew of new fans. Kaede had been watching it on a loop since she got home.

"No lingering attachments here?"

"You asked me once."

"Mm?"

"Why I chose statistical science."

"Oh, yeah. I did."

During their jaunt round Misakiguchi.

"As a gift to the departed, I'll let you know."

"I think you mean parting gift."

He had not yet shuffled off this mortal coil.

"I thought I might figure it out if I came here."

"Figure what out?"

"Who 'everyone' is."

"……"

He reacted with silence, but he'd been thinking the same thing.

"And I thought knowing that would help me understand the girls better."

She grinned sheepishly. And that proved she meant it. She'd never been able to read the room and never quite fit in, even in Sweet Bullet. They'd accepted her despite that. But she wanted to understand them better, if she could. To really get what Nodoka and the other girls were going through. She'd known her happiness wasn't something "everyone" decided, but something she made for herself…but that just made her want to know how the other members defined it. Naturally, it was all tied up in the hope that understanding better would make them even closer.

And as a means to that end, Uzuki had tried to learn more about everyone. To become part of that crowd.

And her goals had aligned with those who resented her for being somebody and wanted to make her just another college girl.

The result? Uzuki had started to share their sensibilities, dress like they did. Have fun talking about the same things. She'd begun reading the room.

To Sakuta's mind, that was the true nature of the Adolescence Syndrome here. Rio might have found a better way to explain it, but this was good enough for him. He didn't need to tackle the ongoing phenomenon—only his friend Uzuki Hirokawa.

"I bet you had a similar reason."

"Mm?"

"For picking statistical science. You knew what I meant, but you're playing dumb."

Uzuki grinned, reading him well.

"Like I said, I just picked the major that seemed the easiest to get into."

"Well, I decided to let you study for both of us. If you figure anything out, lemme know."

"Did you even listen to me?"

"I ignored it on purpose."

She flashed him a broad grin, then got serious.

"I'm glad I got to talk to you one last time, Sakuta."

"Witty repartee *is* always fun."

"Exactly!"

Uzuki glanced down at her phone. She was probably keeping an eye on the time.

"You got work?"

"Yeah, I gotta run."

She held out her hand.

"Oh, Zukki," he said, taking her hand.

A parting handshake.

"……?"

She smiled, waiting for him to finish.

He didn't have the rest ready. He'd only just learned she was leaving school. But his feelings took shape all on their own and spilled right on out.

"Congrats on graduating."

If college was time spent prepping for life in the world at large, then Uzuki was ready to go on her way.

A little faster than the rest, but embarking on a path she'd chosen.

For a moment, she just blinked at him. Then she giggled and looked pleased.

Her hand gripped his. She smiled once more, then said, "I really gotta go," and raced off toward the gate.

The students flooding in saw her going out. They were all dressed like typical college kids again today. Same hair, same backpacks, same makeup, same purses. Talking about the same things, checking the same sites on their phones, listening to the same music on their earphones. Uzuki could drop out, but that wouldn't change. This was their normal.

And Uzuki saw them looking at her.

She saw and didn't let it bother her.

She just kept going full tilt out the gates.

A few steps off campus, she suddenly hit the brakes, like she'd remembered something.

She spun back to look at Sakuta.

"Bye-bye, Sakuta!" she cried, jumping up and down and waving both hands.

This Uzuki couldn't read the room.

But this wasn't a regression. She was undeniably different from her old self.

She'd learned how things went. She knew that people laughed at her. She discovered a part of herself that was willing to laugh at others.

But she would no longer pick up on that in real time.

She didn't notice the students passing her and laughing. Didn't hear them scoffing "So cringe" or "It's too early."

She just kept waving, happily waiting for Sakuta to respond.

So he waved back, just as dramatically.

That earned him some appalled looks, but he didn't care.

Uzuki yelled, "Bye-bye!" again, with a thoroughly satisfied grin. That smile mattered far more to him.

She ran off toward the station, no longer lost.

He watched her go.

Not taking a step until she was out of sight.

It took all of three seconds.

And when the fourth second rolled around, a girl's voice came from his side.

"Aww, such a shame. And after I let her read the room."

There was a woman standing next to him. She looked to be around twenty.

She wore red. But not your typical red. She was dressed like Santa Claus. A miniskirt version, with black tights beneath.

"……"

Sakuta blinked at her a few times, and she caught him looking. She scanned their surroundings, like she was checking something. Sakuta followed her gaze.

"I'm impressed," she said, putting her hand to her lips. A phony gesture. "You can see me."

A cute face. Cutesy body language.

The clock showed eight forty-five AM. Five minutes till first period began. The students headed down the grove were in a hurry.

There must have been fifty or sixty around, but none of them showed any interest in the mystery Santa. That miniskirt should've been impossible to miss. It didn't seem like they were pretending not to notice, either.

They couldn't see her at all.

"I thought you might, Azusagawa."

"…Who are you again?"

He didn't know any Santas.

"Don't worry, this is the first time we've met."

"I have only worries."

She clearly knew him, but if only he could see her…how was he supposed to relax?

"But you do know about me."

"Not that I'm aware of."

"Oh?"

The miniskirt Santa's grin got downright mean.

"I'm Touko Kirishima," she said.

He *did* know that name.

afterword

The college arc begins!

First a TV series, then a movie—the *Rascal* series has had help from so many people and has grown up big and strong. I'm grateful to all the readers who've lent it their power.

I'm deeply indebted to my editors Kurokawa, Yoshida, and Kurosaki during the writing of this volume.

Once again, I must thank readers who stuck with me to the end. *She'll* be in the limelight next time. Look forward to it.

Hajime Kamoshida